An Agreeable Compromise

by

Jann Rowland

One Good Sonnet Publishing
Publishers of Fine Romance
and Fantasy Fiction

By Jann Rowland

Published by One Good Sonnet Publishing:

PRIDE AND PREJUDICE VARIATIONS

An Agreeable Compromise
Unintended Consequences
More Agreeably Engaged
Bonds of Love
Danger at the Netherfield Ball
No Cause to Repine
Among Intimate Acquaintances
In Default of Heirs Male
Prisoner of Longbourn
Bonds of Friendship

AN AGREEABLE COMPROMISE

Copyright © 2022 Jann Rowland

Cover Design by Jann Rowland

Published by One Good Sonnet Publishing

ISBN: 1-989212-99-9
ISBN-13: 978-1-989212-99-8

To my family who have, as always, shown their unconditional love and encouragement.

CHAPTER I

*M*iss Caroline Bingley was going to be a problem.

Darcy knew this instinctively. She was a sister to one of his closest friends, Charles Bingley, a woman of high confidence, a woman forthright and bold. Since Darcy had made her acquaintance two years ago, he had been in no doubt of her ambitions—Miss Bingley believed she was the only choice to become his wife and mistress of all he possessed. Putting aside any consideration for her position in life—that of the daughter of a tradesman—Darcy had never had any affinity for her, had never considered her as anything other than his friend's sister.

But Miss Bingley was nothing if not determined. She flattered and flirted, simpered and smirked, plied him with her brand of allurements, which Darcy was forced to confess, were not inconsiderable. Miss Bingley was not unattractive, being both dark of hair and fair of countenance, perhaps a handsome woman rather than beautiful. Yet, the avarice that always shone in her eyes in his presence, her jealousy for his attention to any other woman, however slight, rendered what should be a pleasing countenance ugly.

Of more importance to Darcy's current situation, Miss Bingley was the mistress of his friend's newly leased estate. As Bingley had asked him to join them to lend his assistance and knowledge of estate management, there was little he could do to avoid her. Thus, armed with the knowledge of her ambitions, Darcy endured her as best he could, parrying her attempts with the lightness and grace of an expert fencer, dodging when that did not work, and retreating when he must. Any other woman might have recognized not only his lack of interest but his active dislike for her. Miss Bingley, however, was not *any* woman.

"Shall I gird you with your foil, Mr. Darcy?" asked Snell, his valet, one morning a few days after his arrival at Netherfield Park. "Or perhaps your cousin, the colonel, will lend you his cavalry saber so you may always have your weapon at hand."

Darcy snorted at his man's dry jest. Just as Miss Bingley was no normal woman, Snell was not a typical manservant. He was a bit of an oddity, fastidious and prickly, though he took care of Darcy with the zeal of a servant of many years. Most valets would not presume to speak so openly in their master's presence; but that was one of Snell's quirks, for he pushed the boundaries between master and servant. Darcy would not think of replacing him, for the man was cool and efficient; there was nothing negative Darcy could say about his diligence.

"A cavalry saber might not be enough," mused Darcy. "Perhaps a lance would do."

The slightest hint of a smile appeared on Snell's face, the most the man ever allowed himself. "A lance is unwieldy when not on horseback. Besides, I do not believe you have trained in its use."

"Perhaps that is so," said Darcy. "Then I suppose I must rely on my wits to thwart Miss Bingley's attempts. Do not concern yourself, Snell—I believe I may safely say that I shall *never* submit to Miss Bingley's attempts to connect herself to me."

"Your staff will rejoice when they hear that, sir."

A few moments later, Darcy left the room to join his friend in the breakfast parlor; that was the one part of the day Darcy knew he would be free of Miss Bingley's cloying attentions, for the woman was not an early riser. It was a misconception, a notion that those of society, since they were often out so late in the evenings during the season, slept late the following morning, and always kept to such late hours, even at their estates. Some did not change their habits, but those diligent in the management of their properties knew mornings were best for conducting the business of the day. If one did not rise until noon, one lost half the day, for the tenants and servants certainly did not stay abed that late.

"Darcy!" greeted Bingley when Darcy stepped into the room.

"Bingley," replied Darcy to his friend. Bingley, though he enjoyed parties and balls until the wee hours of the morning, easily adapted to his new surroundings when in the country. Indeed, Bingley was a man who could adjust to whatever situation in which he found himself. In some ways, Darcy envied him for it.

"Well, my friend?" asked Bingley when he had arranged a plate for himself from the sideboard. "What are your initial impressions of my new home?"

Darcy chewed his food thoughtfully, considering his friend's question. "Netherfield is an excellent investment, Bingley. It is a little neglected, as you can easily see by the problems we have encountered. With care and attention, however, I suspect it will become profitable. The question is whether you wish to settle here."

"That is not something I have considered yet," said Bingley with his typical indifference. "I have been here for less than two weeks, as you know. This is my first foray into estate management, and I do not yet know if it suits me." Bingley paused and grimaced, adding: "As you no doubt understand from Caroline's comments, she does not favor the neighborhood."

"If you will pardon my saying it," replied Darcy, "your sister's opinion, while you should consider it, should not be the basis of your decision. This estate is *your* potential home and that of your future wife. In my opinion, your sister's judgment should influence you but little."

"That is true," replied Bingley. "But her voice is piercing when displeased, and for the nonce, I prefer not to provoke her."

"Understandable," replied Darcy.

"Please allow me to say, Darcy," said Bingley, his manner distinctly uncomfortable, "that I appreciate your willingness to endure Caroline's excesses. I know she can be a trial."

"It is nothing, Bingley," said Darcy, pushing away Bingley's concerns and his own earlier thoughts. "I can handle your sister."

"I dare say you can." Bingley's expression was brimming with mirth. "But I apologize all the same. Caroline has never listened to much that I say, and in the matter of her pursuit of you, her convictions rule her. All my cautions mean nothing to her."

"As I said, Bingley," replied Darcy, "you need not concern yourself."

"Good, good," said Bingley. "There was one other matter of which

I wished to speak to you, for Sir William Lucas of Lucas Lodge has invited us to an assembly the day after tomorrow."

"And I suppose you wish to attend," said Darcy, pushing the stab of vexation aside in favor of humor.

"You know me well enough to know I do," said Bingley. "Besides, my neighbors will expect me to mingle among them, lest they brand me proud and distant."

"Yes, you are correct, Bingley," replied Darcy. "Then I suppose we must attend."

"Shall you dance, Darcy? I know you do not enjoy the activity, but I should like *all* my family and friends to convey a good impression to the community."

"I shall do my duty," said Darcy. "While I will not promise to greet the activity with as much eagerness as you possess, I shall not embarrass you."

"Excellent! Then we shall call it settled."

Indeed, we shall.

Darcy did not look forward to the evening, for not only was he not enamored with dancing, but he also knew Miss Bingley would stalk him the entire night, begging him for his attentions and insulting the locals with equal fervor. Yet he had no choice but to endure it. Bingley was correct—his friend's neighbors *would* expect it of him.

"Well, Charlotte?" asked Elizabeth playfully of her friend. "As you are the daughter of Sir William Lucas, you must have *some* intelligence of our new neighbors. Will you not share?"

Charlotte turned an amused eye on Elizabeth, prompting a laugh in return. A moment's observation already told her a few details of the party that stood before them in the door to the assembly rooms of Meryton. They were three men and two women, one man obviously related to the two women based on his resemblance to them. One of the pair looked upon the company, her nose upturned as if some offensive odor had wafted under her nose, while the other merely appeared bored. Of the gentlemen, one was short and dumpy, with a bulbous nose and a longing gaze toward the refreshments, while the other two were tall and handsome. The shorter of the two had reddish-blond hair and an eager demeanor, while the other was darker and more solemn.

"The two ladies," said Charlotte by her side, "are Mrs. Hurst and Miss Bingley. The elder of the two is the wife of the shorter gentleman, while the younger keeps house for her brother. Mr. Bingley is the man looking at Jane as if seeing a luminous being from heaven for the first time, though he has never had the benefit of an introduction to her."

Elizabeth laughed at her friend's jest, having noticed the man's intrigued looks at her sister herself. "Jane does draw eyes wherever she goes. He appears amiable, and I have always thought she required an amiable husband."

"Your thoughts proceed to matrimony with unseemly haste, Eliza," quipped Charlotte, sending them both into laughter.

"Perhaps they do," said Elizabeth. "But Jane deserves a husband more than any of us, and she has a greater chance, in my estimation."

"You must be correct," replied Charlotte. "But I shall not indulge in speculation at this early date."

"Nor would I ask it of you. What of the other gentleman?"

Charlotte turned to Elizabeth. "Did not your father visit and bring you all word of our new neighbors?"

"You know my father," replied Elizabeth, rolling her eyes at her father's quirks. "He visited Netherfield as any dutiful man might, but he evaded our questions with the expertise of an acrobat."

The laugh with which Charlotte responded bespoke a long acquaintance with Mr. Bennet. "Yes, I suppose he did at that.

"The final member of the Netherfield party is a Mr. Darcy. He is Mr. Bingley's old friend and has come at Mr. Bingley's request to help him become accustomed to his position managing the estate."

"Then Mr. Darcy possesses an estate?" asked Elizabeth.

"A great property in Derbyshire, from what I understand." Charlotte turned a sly glance on Elizabeth. "Perhaps Jane should focus on him, for he is the more consequential man by far. Or perhaps you might attempt to win his approval yourself."

"Shall you not entrap him in *your* web?" asked Elizabeth with a grin. "He might prefer your charms to mine."

"Then a contest it is. I shall anticipate crossing swords with you."

As the night progressed, however, Elizabeth suspected that no one in the neighborhood would capture the elusive Mr. Darcy. For one, the man did not seem to enjoy himself, stalking about the floor as he did, rarely dancing. When he did dance, he stood up with Miss Bingley—though Elizabeth noted his dour countenance when he did so—and Mrs. Hurst. He also favored Jane with a set and danced once with Charlotte, for which Elizabeth was certain to tease her friend. The rest of the evening, however, he avoided the dancing, and one of his party, in particular.

That person, unfortunately, could not seem to understand his aversion to her company. Miss Bingley, Elizabeth had noted from the first moment of her arrival, disdained the gathering in which she found herself, her contemptuous glares and haughty demeanor clear to anyone who cared to look. To Mr. Darcy, she directed all her efforts, unaware that the gentleman could not tolerate her.

"Mr. Darcy!" exclaimed the woman with more eagerness than sense later in the evening in Elizabeth's hearing. "How fortunate I am to have found you, for there is no one in this company who is worth my time."

"It would be best if you did not speak in such a manner or with such volume," replied Mr. Darcy, his jaw clenching, showing his frustration in the bulging muscles of his face. "You would not wish to offend your brother's neighbors."

"It is of no consequence," replied Miss Bingley, her manner as airy as her lack of understanding. She seemed to catch sight of Elizabeth at that moment and turned to address her. "Miss Eliza Bennet, as I recall. What do you do there? Are you attempting to overhear our conversation?"

"If I have," said Elizabeth, "it is through no fault of mine. I have been standing here for the last five minutes complete. Perhaps it would be best if you would guard your tongue and retain your awareness of your surroundings, for it is not my fault you spoke in such an unguarded fashion as you did in my hearing."

Miss Bingley regarded her with a look of such heat that Elizabeth thought it might scorch her. At that moment, however, Mr. Darcy chose to intervene.

"Miss Elizabeth, will you do me the honor of standing up the next with me?"

Ignoring all Miss Bingley's displeasure, Elizabeth assented and accepted his arm. It was fortunate the next sets were about to start, for she did not think she could continue to endure Miss Bingley with equanimity.

Darcy had no great opinion of the company in which he found himself. At the same time, he was also not in the habit of insulting new acquaintances to their faces with no attempt to disguise his words.

The longer the night had progressed, the more frustrated Darcy had become with Miss Bingley, for the woman would not—perhaps could not—understand his disinclination for her company. She persisted in spite of everything he did to avoid her. Should he lose his temper and reprimand her, informing her in the strongest of terms that he had no interest in what she had to offer, Darcy doubted he would deter her in the slightest. The woman was single-minded, intent upon her prey, allowing nothing to stand in her way.

In some ways, Darcy knew he had done Miss Elizabeth a disservice. The woman did not deserve the vitriol he knew Miss Bingley would fling at her. Yet, even the little observation Darcy had indulged in her informed him that Miss Elizabeth was a woman equal to the task, one who would not quail in the face of all Miss Bingley's displeasure. His request to her he had made on the spur of the moment, frustrated as he was by Miss Bingley's vitriolic behavior. But he soon found himself enjoying his time with Miss Elizabeth, for she appeared to be a bright woman, easy of conversation and magnetic of person.

"I apologize, Miss Elizabeth," Darcy found it necessary to say after they had danced for some few moments. "Miss Bingley had no right to say what she did. I regret her behavior."

"It appears to me, Mr. Darcy," replied Miss Elizabeth, "that you should not bear the responsibility of apologizing, for you were not uncivil."

Darcy nodded. "I am of a reticent character. Sometimes my behavior will lead others to assume I am proud or to take offense. But I am never purposefully discourteous."

"I would never have accused you of it," replied Elizabeth. "For what it is worth, I accept your words and acquit you of any part of Miss Bingley's rudeness. However, I shall reserve my acceptance of an apology for when Miss Bingley herself deigns to offer it."

By the side of the floor, Darcy glimpsed Miss Bingley watching them, her eyes narrowed as she glared at Miss Elizabeth. His partner was aware of Miss Bingley's scrutiny, but it was equally obvious that she cared nothing for the woman's opinion. Darcy cared little himself, so he put her out of his mind, though he knew he may need to have a word with her to prevent her from further comments designed to insult her brother's neighbors.

"Then, if you are willing, I believe I should prefer to leave this objectionable subject."

Miss Elizabeth's eyes danced with mirth. "It would appall Miss Bingley to learn that you called her an 'objectionable subject.'"

"On the contrary, Miss Elizabeth," said Darcy, enjoying their banter, "I doubt she would give the notion any credence, even if I told her myself."

The tinkling laughter with which she responded lightened Darcy's heart. "I agree, sir. Let us speak of something else."

"What of books?" asked Darcy. "Do you read? Shall we not compare our opinions?"

"Some might say that it is not appropriate to discuss books in a ballroom," replied Miss Elizabeth. "But I am not one of those."

They set to it with a will, amusing each other for the rest of their time together. Their tastes were not identical, though Darcy noted something of a similarity in their turns of thought. Darcy was more widely read than she, unsurprising given his formal education at Eton, and then Cambridge. Miss Elizabeth, however, was an erudite young woman for her age and position in life, having read far more of the same material than he might have expected.

What also became clear soon after was that her thoughts on the material she read were mature, her opinions clearly stated and well-considered. Again, their conclusions were not always the same but were similar in many respects, their opinions not unalike. Furthermore, when they disagreed, Miss Elizabeth possessed the quickness to argue her viewpoints intelligently, in many ways, her manner of expressing herself as articulate as a champion debater. Where they disagreed, she was more than willing to allow his opinion if he argued it well, and she never attempted to disparage. By the end of their time together, Darcy found he had never been entertained half so well in the ballroom.

"Well, Mr. Darcy?" asked she as she accepted his hand and allowed him to escort her to the side of the dance floor. "Have I proved to you that I am naught but a bluestocking?"

"No, indeed," replied Darcy. "It is clear you are intelligent enough to be one, but I suspect you are simply confident in your conclusions and not afraid to defend your opinion."

"Then I thank you for that bit of flattery, sir," replied she. "My father has raised me to be inquisitive, and among my sisters, I am closest to him in character."

Darcy regarded her with interest. "I assume your father visited my friend, but I had not yet arrived. I should like an introduction to him when the occasion permits."

"That can be arranged." She grinned at him and curtseyed. "For the moment, however, I believe I must retreat. If I do not, scenes might arise unpleasant to all."

With those words, she turned and moved away, Darcy watching her as she left. His contemplation of her person was why he did not recognize the danger, the import of her words occurring to him only after Miss Bingley accosted him.

"What an excellent gentleman you are, Mr. Darcy," cooed the woman, inserting her person far too close to him for comfort. "Giving attention to those unworthy is the hallmark of a gentleman. But I cannot but suppose you are relieved to be free of Miss Elizabeth's uncouth company."

To say anything at all would be to invite her to despise Miss Elizabeth more than she already did. As such, Darcy eschewed it, looking for a means of escape. So, the interminable evening continued.

Had it not been so very pathetic, the scene might have diverted Elizabeth. Then again, her diversion would have been for Miss Bingley's behavior, not for Mr. Darcy's plight. Their dance had opened her eyes to the gentleman's worth, and Elizabeth wanted to know more of him. But it was equally obvious that she could not contemplate it, not if she wished to remain unscathed from Miss Bingley's poison.

"What an interesting evening this has been, Lizzy," said Charlotte later that evening. Charlotte, Elizabeth noticed, had watched the dance of evasion between Mr. Darcy and Miss Bingley with as much amusement as Elizabeth had. "You have made an important conquest. Shall I quit the field now before I am mortified by your utter victory?"

"By my count," replied Elizabeth, "we have both danced with Mr. Darcy once."

"Ah, but banal conversation interspersed with long periods of silence characterized my dance with him. If you and Mr. Darcy were silent more than ten seconds together, it would surprise me to learn of it."

"One dance does not a marriage make."

"No, I suppose it does not." Charlotte grinned. "Else Miss Bingley might have ordered her trousseau long before coming to Netherfield."

Elizabeth could not restrain the laughter that forced its way from her breast. "Yes, I suppose she would have." Elizabeth paused to regard the woman, who was even now making her way around the floor pursuing Mr. Darcy, who had moved that way. "It is astonishing how little she understands Mr. Darcy."

"Rather, I suspect she simply does not wish to understand," said Charlotte.

"Yes, I suppose you must be correct. For my part, I would wager the gentleman is more than equal to the challenge of avoiding her snares."

"Aye, he does seem to possess the necessary stamina."

Elizabeth turned to Charlotte. "I must own I am surprised that she has so much opportunity to pursue Mr. Darcy. As a man, he may choose whether he wishes to dance. But she is not so fortunate. I might have thought our fine men of the neighborhood would brave her displeasure."

"There you would be incorrect," replied Charlotte, barely concealing her humor. "Earlier this evening, one of our intrepid men did just that. As it was after her dance with Mr. Darcy, Miss Bingley declared she would not dance again that evening. Rumors of her unwillingness made their way around the room quickly, and now no one bothers her."

Elizabeth shook her head in disgust. "She does not appear to understand what a poor impression she is making on her new neighbors."

"I am certain she simply does not care, Lizzy."

"With that, I must concur."

On and on it went. Elizabeth danced as much as was her wont, yet she saw much of the intricate series of thrusts and parries between Mr. Darcy and Miss Bingley. The man avoided her, hiding behind those who wished to speak to her, walking away when he could, avoiding her by speaking to other gentlemen in the room, though he did not appear to enjoy their company. He did not dance again, but Elizabeth did not fault him, as Miss Bingley gave him no opportunity to repeat the gambit he had played when he had asked her to dance.

It was an unfortunate coincidence that led Miss Bingley to finally corner her prey in a place where Elizabeth could not fail to overhear their ensuing conversation. This time, however, Miss Bingley did not deign to notice her, and Elizabeth determined not to draw the unpleasant woman's attention.

"The night is waning Mr. Darcy," said she, uncaring as to the volume of her voice. "Soon, we shall be free to quit this miserable place and return to Netherfield, inadequate though it is."

"There is nothing wrong with Netherfield, Miss Bingley," replied Mr. Darcy, seeking some means of escape. "It fits your brother's need for the present."

"It is a hovel," snorted Miss Bingley in a most unladylike fashion. "And given it is the best house in the community, I shudder to consider the squalor in which the rest of these *gentlefolk* subsist."

Mr. Darcy did not respond. Miss Bingley was not of a mind to allow his silence.

"Come, Mr. Darcy. I know you must long to unleash your opinions of this gathering. You should not think to demur, for my opinion will coincide with yours in every particular."

"As I have said before, I espouse no such feelings."

"Yet your every action, your every glance confirms it! You think no more of these insignificant people than I do. Look at them! What presumption these people possess to aspire to a level they can in no way inhabit. I am certain you must agree."

"People, Miss Bingley," said Mr. Darcy, "are similar no matter where you go. You call these people coarse, but they are no worse than any others I have seen in many other communities."

With that, the gentleman found his opening and slipped through, Miss Bingley chasing him much as she had most of the evening. They left Elizabeth to contemplate what she had heard, and she was uncertain what to make of it. She had seen and heard enough to suppose that Mr. Darcy did not agree with all of Miss Bingley's opinions on the matter, but his final words in her hearing suggested he was not devoid of pride himself.

Uncertain, Elizabeth pushed the matter from her mind for the moment. There was little enough to be gained from exasperating herself against either, so she did not attempt it.

CHAPTER II

nfortunately for Elizabeth's peace of mind, her thoughts of Mr. Darcy did not fade as she might have wished. Overall, she reflected in the darkness of her room that evening after the assembly, she had obtained the impression of an excellent gentleman, one intelligent and estimable. He could not, in any way, be called a warm man, though the extent of his civility might be in question. The words he had spoken to Miss Bingley stayed with her, taunting her with the suggestion his true opinions had been other than what he had revealed to her. Yet, at the same time, she knew his comment may have been benign, an attempt to satisfy a woman he found distasteful.

These thoughts persisted into the next morning, and while her sisters had no conception of Elizabeth's quiet attitude, her father was perceptive enough to have deduced something was amiss. Elizabeth had always esteemed her father as a sensible man, one on whom she could count when she experienced a problem for which she had no answer, or on whom she could lay her burdens to gain clarity. In such a situation as this, his support was a boon.

"These are troubling accounts, indeed," said he after Elizabeth explained her experiences from the previous evening. "Mr. Darcy's faults are heavy, and the less said of Miss Bingley, the better."

"Oh, Papa," said Elizabeth, a familiar refrain between them. "How you do carry on. I said nothing of Mr. Darcy's faults. I merely wish to understand the gentleman better."

"You do," said Mr. Bennet, eying her with some interest. "Dare I suggest I detect a hint of significance in your manner beyond what is usual for a new acquaintance?"

Elizabeth could not help her glance skyward; while her father was her confidante, his sardonic sense of humor often exasperated her. "If you wish to tease my confusion, perhaps I should just retreat from the battlefield now before you embarrass me beyond endurance."

The chuckle with which Mr. Bennet responded signaled his capitulation. "No, Lizzy my dear, I should never dream of trying to sport with your intelligence. Unlike my dearly departed wife, you are no easy mark."

"One might question your abilities if you only focus your fire on easy marks," jibed Elizabeth.

Mr. Bennet grinned, then returned his attention to Elizabeth's account. "What you have told me of this Mr. Darcy suggests a character not unlike mine yet possessing a position in society which requires his diligence. That I do not possess such a legacy to protect is a matter of some relief, for we Bennets have never been prominent enough to warrant such expenditures of effort."

"No, I suppose it does not."

"Your mother, were she alive today, would have latched onto these two gentlemen in our midst and proclaimed they were her salvation. That she would have expected them to offer for her eldest daughters and make them happy would be of secondary consideration, for their ability to provide for her in her dotage was of utmost importance."

To this, Elizabeth decided there was no need to comment. Elizabeth's memories of her mother were few and indistinct, for the woman had perished when Elizabeth had been five years of age, expiring during her attempt to bring her fifth child into the world, the child joining her in death. Her father often spoke of his wife in such terms, and from Elizabeth's memories, she had been a woman of little sense and less understanding. With spotty memories such as these, there was no reason for her to disparage the woman who had given her life.

"But that is beside the point, I suppose," said Mr. Bennet, giving her a wry smile. "I have digressed, and I apologize, Lizzy. If you want my opinion, I suggest you do not attempt to read any meaning into Mr. Darcy's comment that is not readily apparent."

Elizabeth felt easier upon hearing that his opinion agreed with hers.

"I spoke to your gentleman a little last night," observed Mr. Bennet.

Regarding him with curiosity, Elizabeth said: "Mr. Darcy suggested he had never made your acquaintance."

"Then he must have informed you of that before," said Mr. Bennet. "It was near the end of the evening, and seeing how he fled from that harpy his friend calls a sister, I requested an introduction."

"That would account for the discrepancy," said Elizabeth. "What did you think of him?"

"Much as I have already told you, my dear. Mr. Darcy is withdrawn and not eager to mingle, faults with which I may readily identify myself. But he also seemed a good sort of fellow, one with whom I could engage in a conversation of more importance than the weather or share a game of chess without becoming bored with him much sooner than I should."

"Then I shall accept your suggestion," said Elizabeth. "I had no wish to believe that Mr. Darcy was dissembling, and every instinct informed me he spoke for reasons other than censure."

"Excellent, Lizzy. I hope you come to esteem him, for I wish to know him and his friend better. Though the rest of the party may not be agreeable, I suspect Mr. Bingley and Mr. Darcy will be well worth knowing."

When Charlotte came later that morning for a visit, she found all four Bennet sisters in the sitting-room. Jane had met with the housekeeper that morning and had returned to join her sisters as they sewed clothes for the tenant children. While Jane and Mary attended to their business with diligence, their fingers working their expertise over the fabric, Elizabeth's efforts were decidedly slower, her progress gained more by determination than skill—Elizabeth had never been one to enjoy the activity. The youngest sister, Kitty, took part in their endeavors, but she was even less apt than Elizabeth, her creations inspected meticulously by her sisters to ensure the quality of the work. Kitty was still young, being only seventeen. She played the pianoforte passably and was the only sister to have any interest in art. She was also the sister most likely to shirk her studies for idleness, complaining of the boredom she might have eased by a more active philosophy. She was a good girl, but at times Elizabeth found her trying.

"Well, Jane," said Charlotte when she settled into their midst, the Bennet sisters having put aside their sewing with little regret, "it seems you made an important conquest last night."

"I have no notion of what you speak," replied Jane, though it was clear to them all that she knew exactly to what Charlotte referred. Jane, a reticent creature though she was, had never been in the habit of embarrassment, though the attention she received from gentlemen wherever she went was often marked.

"Why, Mr. Bingley's attentions!" exclaimed Charlotte. "I declare the man had no eyes for anyone else last night, for he danced twice with you and no other, and often stood with you when not engaged in dancing."

"I will remind you, Charlotte," said Jane, unperturbed by their friend's teasing, "that my acquaintance with Mr. Bingley comprises one evening at a ball. It is too soon for anything to have developed between us, even were Mr. Bingley the most impulsive man alive."

"Ah, Jane," said Charlotte with no little affection, "you make it difficult to tease you when you respond thus."

"I have had plenty of practice, for you and Lizzy train your fire on me without mercy."

"Kitty and I are pleased they do," said Mary, smiling at her eldest sister. "For it spares us much of their wit."

"What did you think of the Bingleys?" asked Kitty before anyone could say anything else.

"The same as any of you, I expect," replied Charlotte. "Mr. Bingley was everything amiable, though his sisters were clearly not cut from the same cloth."

"Oh, without a doubt," said Elizabeth, not surprised at all by her friend's comment, given their conversations the previous evening. "Miss Bingley spent the entire evening chasing Mr. Darcy, and Mrs. Hurst appeared disinclined to speak much to anyone."

"And the less said about her husband, the better," added Kitty.

"I found Miss Bingley pleasing, though I will own that I did not speak with her much."

Jane's comment surprised no one, though it was equally unsurprising when she said nothing to rebut Kitty's comment about Mr. Hurst. Jane was, at heart, a peacemaker, one who looked for the best in others. She was not blind to poor behavior, but she was less inclined to speak of it than her friends and sisters. Knowing she would not change her sister's opinion regardless of what she said, Elizabeth refrained from saying anything on the subject.

"What of Mr. Darcy?" asked Mary. "Jane, Elizabeth, you danced with him."

"So did Charlotte," observed Elizabeth.

"Mr. Darcy is an excellent man, I suspect," said Charlotte. "He is not the same as Mr. Bingley, to be certain."

"It was difficult to determine what sort of man he is," said Elizabeth, considering what she heard him say the previous evening. "Miss Bingley's continual attempts to engage him did not allow for much insight into his character."

"He is a prominent man, or so I understand," said Charlotte.

"Given his mode of dress and the manners I observed, I am not surprised," said Elizabeth. "What do you know of his situation in life, Charlotte? Other than what you informed me last night, of course."

"Little more than you as to the specifics," replied her friend. "But I heard it rumored about the assembly hall that he owns a great estate in Derbyshire and has connections to an earl."

"That much is true, for I overheard it myself."

Elizabeth looked to Mary with interest, for Mary was the Bennet sister least likely to indulge in gossip, which was saying much, as they all eschewed the practice. Receiving her sisters' looks with some asperity, Mary huffed her displeasure.

"No, I did not gossip. But I was nearby when Miss Bingley boasted of Mr. Darcy's position as the nephew of an earl."

It must have been one of the few times the entire evening that Miss Bingley had not been chasing Mr. Darcy, from what Elizabeth had seen. Of course, it was no surprise the woman would wish to crow about her acquaintance with such a man to the savages that inhabited the neighborhood in which she now resided. No doubt Miss Bingley had implied how *close* her friendship with Mr. Darcy was, ignoring the man's obvious disinclination for her company.

When Kitty made that exact observation, Mary winced, but she did not refrain from answering. "You know I dislike gossip, Kitty. But I shall not say you are incorrect. Miss Bingley was as self-congratulatory as you suggest."

"What a woman!" said Elizabeth. "How anyone could persist in the face of such indifference is beyond astonishing."

"That is not precisely kind, Lizzy," reprimanded Jane.

"I did not intend it to be kind or unkind," replied Elizabeth. "I only spoke the truth of my observation."

Even Jane could find no answer for that, and she did not make the attempt. Charlotte then turned the conversation aside.

"Perhaps Miss Bingley is as you suggest, and perhaps Mr. Darcy does not favor her—I saw nothing to dispute your observation. I will say that I expect they will, for the most part, be excellent neighbors. Mr. Bingley alone makes it certain."

"My father suggested he also found Mr. Darcy estimable," said Elizabeth, remembering his advice to avoid judging the gentleman too harshly.

"I suspect he will prove himself," replied Charlotte.

"If he can protect himself from Miss Bingley's depredations," chimed in Kitty.

"Oh, without a doubt," said Elizabeth. "I might expect Mr. Bingley to control his sister if she was not so very determined."

"And if he could wrest his focus from our Jane!" added Charlotte.

The ladies laughed together, and they spent the rest of their time together in gentle teasing of Longbourn's eldest daughter. Jane was just as impervious as ever, but that did not deter them in the slightest.

Had Darcy known of the conversation at Longbourn that morning, it would have diverted him to no end. Then again, he would also have learned of Miss Elizabeth's uncertainty regarding his comments the previous evening, and having had no intention of offense, he would have been mortified.

Darcy remained unaware of such things, though his thoughts were not on what was happening around him. It should be no surprise to anyone, least of all Darcy, who had known and disdained Miss Bingley for the previous two years, that the woman was engaged in her favorite activity. Or one of her favorites, Darcy amended to himself, for she had several unsavory habits in which she was prone to indulge. Among those, he particularly detested her ability to attack perceived rivals for his favor, congratulate herself on her fortunate situation, overestimate her worth in the world, and speak with contempt about those whose situation in life was superior to her own.

Thus, it was no trouble at all for Darcy to ignore her, and there was little chance of her detecting his inattention. Miss Bingley had, for some reason unfathomable to Darcy, long thought his opinions mirrored her own. The way she pontificated about the neighborhood bespoke her utter confidence in his agreement; she did not even pause to consider whether he was even attending her. In fact, had she any notion of the tenor of his thoughts, she would not have been nearly so sanguine. Then again, she likely would have found some way to tell herself it was not what she thought, while her plotting would have begun in earnest.

Darcy's thoughts at that moment centered on the woman whose acquaintance he had made the previous evening. While Darcy had danced with Miss Bennet and thought her an excellent woman, he had paid little attention to her and did not find her truly interesting. Her younger sister, however . . . .

There was much to appreciate in Miss Elizabeth Bennet. From her deep chestnut locks to the flawless smoothness of her skin to the intelligence shining from her beautiful dark eyes, Darcy did not think he had met such a woman in all his life. While the first stirrings of love did not yet flutter within his breast, Darcy was intrigued by her, wanting to know more of the woman who could debate the intricacies of Milton and not lose her steps or place in the dance. Indeed, Darcy could imagine many debates with her, each more delightful than the last. In Miss Elizabeth's company, one could never find ennui. Such a fate was unfathomable.

And yet, to have such thoughts this early in his acquaintance with her was not only surprising, but Darcy was not certain it was wise. For all her appeal — and Darcy had only a single night on which to base his opinion — she was the daughter of a minor country gentleman, of scant consequence in the world. Could he turn his attention on such a woman when he had the hope of so much more?

Such thoughts could do nothing more than cause him mirth. Miss Elizabeth of little consequence in the world? Even after only a single evening's acquaintance, he could not imagine it. She was limited only by her circumstances, by the fetters binding her to a small neighborhood. Surely, if she were unleashed upon the world at large, she would write a story so vast and compelling that no one would ever dare suggest she was of little importance. All it would take, Darcy thought, was a commitment to expose and polish the gem, to allow it to shine. She would do the rest by her very nature.

And what of Bingley? While his sister droned on, Bingley appeared as lost in his thoughts as Darcy was himself. It took little insight to determine the thrust of Bingley's reminiscences, for he had been as profoundly — and more visibly — impacted by his own experiences last night. While Miss Bennet was not a woman to interest Darcy to any great degree, she was the sort of woman Bingley would find irresistible. If she proved as genuine as she had seemed the previous evening, Bingley might even have found his perfect mate; but that would draw its own trouble.

"In short, they are nothing." Miss Bingley's peculiar droning voice caught and held Darcy's attention. "There is little fashion in them, their society is irksome, their pretension to gentility laughable. If this estate to which you have tied yourself for the next year was not inadequate, the community in which it rests certainly *is*."

Bingley made no response to his sister's denunciation. Unless Darcy missed his guess, Bingley had not even heard. True to her character, Miss Bingley did not realize her brother was not attending her.

"And perhaps the worst among them are the Bennets."

Bingley instantly proved Darcy's suppositions wrong. "What can you mean, Caroline? There is nothing the matter with the Bennets."

"*Everything* is wrong with the Bennets," retorted Miss Bingley. "Why, I have rarely seen such a family as they, all pretense and no substance. All four sisters out at once, their mother taking no interest in guiding them as she ought, and the father a misanthropic waste of a man."

"I must own that you have me at sea, Caroline," said Bingley, when it appeared Mrs. Hurst wished to interject. "Did you exchange even two words with Mr. Bennet last night?"

Miss Bingley glared at him and muttered something about feathers, which allowed her sister to interject.

"The Bennet sisters' mother has passed, Caroline," said Mrs. Hurst. "Apparently, she perished at the youngest girl's birth."

Darcy had already known Miss Bingley would feel no shame at her misstep, so her lack of consideration did not surprise him. He doubted she even realized what an error she had made.

"That is my point," insisted she. "Mr. Bennet has abrogated his responsibilities as a father, for they do not display the delicacy they should as daughters of a supposed gentleman. He should have remarried or contracted a woman to teach them what they must know."

"You are hard on them!" exclaimed Bingley. "Especially when you know nothing of their situation. How do you know they did not have a governess?"

"Anyone who witnesses their behavior cannot help but know!" spat Miss Bingley.

"And yet, I saw nothing wrong with them," asserted Bingley. "They all appeared genteel to me, for there was nothing amiss with their behavior."

Miss Bingley made an unpleasant and guttural sound in the back of her throat, akin to the feral growl of a dog. Darcy wondered if she even recognized her habit. Surely she would have quashed it if she did, for it was most unladylike.

"It is another example of your eagerness to attribute every virtue to any pretty woman, Brother. Miss Bennet is the most insipid woman I have ever met; Miss Mary, a bluestocking; Miss Kitty wild; and Miss Elizabeth, a determined flirt and social climber. What a family!"

While he did not think she intended to betray any particular scorn for Miss Elizabeth, Darcy saw something in her behavior he did not like, beyond his usual objections to anything she said. The previous evening, he had used Miss Elizabeth's proximity to escape Miss Bingley for a time. When he had done it, he had not given it any significant consideration, given no thought to the notion it may make Miss Bingley an enemy of Miss Elizabeth. It appeared Miss Bingley *had*.

It would, without question, invite greater misbehavior on Miss Bingley's part if he attempted to learn anything more about the young woman who had fired his imagination. Darcy at once determined he would not desist for two reasons. The first was that he was not about to allow Miss Bingley's opinion to form his decisions about *anything*, particularly a matter which possessed the potential to bring him happiness in life. The second was his conviction that Miss Elizabeth could withstand any manner of misconduct from Miss Bingley and remain unaffected. Miss Bingley could do all she wished, and he had no doubt Miss Elizabeth would best her time and again.

"The Bennets are an excellent family," said Bingley, his tone unusually firm. "They are also my closest neighbors and foremost among this community's residents. I do not require you to esteem them, Caroline, for your opinion is your own. What I do require is your civility."

"Are you suggesting I do not know how to behave?" demanded Miss Bingley.

"Given what I am seeing now, it seems you do not."

The siblings glared at each other for a long moment. It was a surprise when Miss Bingley looked away first. That she looked at Darcy was not.

"Mr. Darcy, I am certain, agrees with me." It had always astonished Darcy that she expected his agreement, though, to his recollection, he had never done so openly. "It would be in every way insufferable to give consequence to such people. We would be better to avoid them as much as possible."

"There is a fallacy in your thinking, Miss Bingley," said Darcy. He had long since given up attempting to soften his words to her, for he knew she would hear what she wished, regardless. "Your brother now lives in this community, and he is tied to these people for the next year. A landowner who does not foster good relations with others around him is asking for trouble."

"Another year and we will be gone," snapped Miss Bingley. "Their opinions do not signify."

"There you are incorrect, Caroline," said Bingley. "As you know but have endeavored to forget, the lease carries an option to purchase."

"This estate is by no means sufficient," replied she. "We shall leave when the lease has expired."

Bingley's gaze hardened. "I shall remind you that *my* name is on the lease, and it is *my* decision. Such behavior as this will not result in my attending any advice you might wish to impart."

"It is not that, Brother," said Miss Bingley, waving her misstep away like the smoke of a cigar. "I *know* you. This place will not satisfy you. When a year has passed, you will be as eager to leave as I am."

"Perhaps that is true," replied Bingley. "But the fact remains that I shall not suffer your poor behavior toward our neighbors. Moderate your comments concerning them and maintain your civility, or you may depart from Netherfield with the Hursts or go north to our family."

Had Darcy not already had ample proof of her aspirations with respect to the vacant position as his wife, her glance at him showing how unpalatable leaving Netherfield was to her would have informed him of much. As it was, he already knew it all and was not surprised in the slightest.

"You mistake me, Brother," said Miss Bingley with a superior sniff. "I shall not falter, even when confronted by the savagery to which they will expose us every day we remain here. I am not made of stuff so brittle as this."

"As long as you remember yourself, I shall be content," said Bingley, losing interest in her.

From there, the conversation became more desultory, a relief from the denunciations of the previous minutes. The way Miss Bingley watched Darcy and her brother, he wondered what she saw in them, as well as what she meant to do about what her observation told her. Here, in a sleepy little community, the right circumstances existed to undo all her dreams of advancement in society. She would bear careful watching.

Darcy made a mental note to speak with Snell again about maintaining his vigilance. That Snell would not shirk, he understood, but his man could not possibly know about the unmistakable threat to Miss Bingley's designs. Darcy never let his guard down for a moment in Miss Bingley's company, but a little extra help could not go amiss.

CHAPTER III

"*I* am most distressed, Sister. This visit is not proceeding as I had designed."

That was an understatement. As Louisa Hurst had not espoused similar expectations as her sister, not being nearly so blind to the truth as Caroline, it did not surprise her in the slightest.

The problem was, she reflected, that Caroline was so focused on her selfish desires that she was helpless to see what must be obvious to everyone around her. That or she simply did not wish to confess it. And Caroline was more than capable of drawing Louisa into her intrigues.

Caroline had always been the forceful sister, while Louisa had been calmer, more in control of her emotions. Caroline led their intrigues and Louisa followed, willingly or no. Louisa would not call herself a follower precisely—she was as capable of thoughts and motivations as any other, and if she did not agree with her sister, she did not give Caroline as much support as she thought. Yet Caroline was of such a disposition that abhorred being contradicted; it was almost always easier to allow Caroline her head and avoid an argument.

In this instance, however, with Caroline pacing the sitting-room looking for a way to turn Mr. Darcy to her and claim his fortune and position in society—Louisa knew her sister had no care for the man himself—to allow her to do as she wished might be disastrous. Mr. Darcy was not a vindictive man. Would he allow a woman such as Caroline to force his hand? Louisa did not believe he would. It was more likely he would dare all that Caroline could do, regardless of whatever success she had insinuating herself into his life, or—horrific thought though it was—if she managed a compromise.

Did Caroline have it in herself to behave that way? Louisa considered her sister, noting her incoherent mutterings, the way she shook her head, and her single-minded focus on her goal. If Caroline did not have it within her to do *anything* to achieve her ends, Louisa did not know who did. There was little enough Louisa could do to stop her; Caroline had never listened.

"I had thought," said Caroline abruptly, as if her thoughts had coalesced at that moment, "this would be the perfect opportunity to show Mr. Darcy my excellent qualities. Surely, he cannot resist me when I prove to him how adept I am with the management of this house, how perfectly I will fit into his life."

Privately, Louisa was certain Mr. Darcy's primary wishes in a companion were not those things that Caroline valued so highly. If they *were*, Louisa thought he might have given her a closer look, for an alliance with Caroline would not be without benefits, even for a man in Mr. Darcy's position.

"Still, he resists," continued Caroline. "What more must I do to prove myself to him?"

"He just does not seem interested in you, Caroline," said Louisa, trying to cling to tact while informing her sister of the reality of her pretensions without causing a gale in response. "If he was, do you not think he would have shown it?"

"Nonsense," muttered Caroline, continuing her pacing. "There must be something I am missing, something I can do to make my qualities clear."

Louisa sighed, regretting again her sister's unfortunate ability to believe what she wished. "From what I can see, Mr. Darcy does not see you that way."

"You are wrong," spat Caroline. "I am his perfect mate."

"Did the way he did everything he could to avoid you at the assembly tell you nothing? It is time for this delusion to end, Caroline. Mr. Darcy has no wish to have you for a wife."

"I care not," growled Caroline. "Mr. Darcy will have me one way or another. I have invested more than two years into my campaign to elicit his proposal. I shall not give up now when success is in my grasp."

"Then you shall do it without my help," said Louisa standing to glare at her sister.

"You would betray me now?" demanded Caroline.

"It is no betrayal, Caroline," rejoined Louisa. "Listen to what you are saying. Do you propose to ignore Mr. Darcy's wishes and force your way into his home and life?"

"I mean to do what I must to ensure our family gains the respect of society as our father wished."

Louisa shook her head in dismay. "Papa did not wish to ascend to society's heights by any means necessary. He wished to join the landed class, but he was not blind to decency."

"Neither am I," said Caroline. "I shall have Mr. Darcy, Louisa. You will see. He cannot resist my appeal. Of that, I am certain."

There was little enough to say to such blindness. Louisa did not know what Caroline meant to do, but she would have no part in it. She could only hope her sister did not ruin them all forever.

Wary of being observed, Darcy backed away from the door to the sitting-room, which was standing ajar, and made his way down the hallway toward the stairs. Understanding such weighty information required the privacy of his room. Anything else and Darcy might betray his knowledge of what Miss Bingley had said, and that might prove a goad to provoke the woman to rise to the level of insanity her words suggested.

Once Darcy gained his room, he eased himself into an armchair before the merrily crackling fire, wondering what he should do. The thought of informing Bingley of what he had overheard was appealing, but Darcy did not know if it was the right way to handle the situation. Might Mrs. Hurst tell her brother? Darcy could not be certain, but he thought she would not, preferring to disengage from her sister and allow her to do as she would. In a certain sense, Darcy understood her feelings.

After perhaps fifteen minutes of considering the matter, attacking it from every angle he could imagine, Darcy decided against speaking to Bingley. For one, he did not wish to put his friend in a difficult position, especially when he could not know if Miss Bingley's words were mere bluster or a sign of deceit. Darcy suspected he knew, but he could not be certain. His second reason was his desire to avoid provoking Miss Bingley to greater heights of folly. As it stood, she considered her success inevitable, or at the very least, attainable. If he did not awaken her to his knowledge of her schemes, that may prevent her from actions that she could not recant.

At that moment, Snell came into the room, carrying a jacket and a brush. Darcy considered his man and then called Snell to attend him, which he did without question.

"What do you propose, Mr. Darcy?" asked the valet when Darcy explained what he had learned.

"For the moment, nothing," said Darcy. There was no reason to inform Snell of his reasons, he knew, for his servant did not require it. "I wished you to know of it so you may remain vigilant."

"Of course," said Snell. "I do not wish to have Miss Bingley as a mistress any more than you want her as your wife."

"Good man," said Darcy. "While I cannot say if Miss Bingley will act in a manner she should not, it seems, from what she said, that she has not dismissed the notion altogether."

"If she has not," muttered Snell, "she has never contended with *me*."

Darcy did not think his valet had intended him to overhear, so he elected to ignore it. "I shall take care as well."

"That much is certain, Mr. Darcy. I shall inform you if I hear anything from the servants. Now, if you will excuse me."

Darcy waved him away, and Snell departed with the jacket and the brush. Darcy rose, intending to seek out his friend.

Finding Bingley was a simple matter, and at his friend's suggestion, Darcy agreed to a ride out on the estate. Netherfield was a picturesque property, with gently rolling hills and pleasing strands of trees amid the glory of her fields. It was late enough in the year that the harvest was complete, the fields barren, waiting until the following year and the planting for life to return.

The friends thundered along the pastures and woods of Netherfield, enjoying the freedom of the wind in their hair, and the sun on their faces. They rode with no true destination in mind, hurdling obstacles and crying out their joy in freedom from restraint.

When they had ridden perhaps half an hour, they came to a long meadow bordered by trees and a long fence. Darcy identified it at once as the border between Netherfield and Longbourn to the west. There, a rider came into view on the other side. It was Mr. Bennet.

"Mr. Bingley. Mr. Darcy," called Mr. Bennet in greeting when they came close enough to hail each other.

"Mr. Bennet," said Bingley with his typical enthusiasm. "How fortunate we are to have found you."

"Is that so?" asked Mr. Bennet with what Darcy suspected was a typical turn of amusement. "How so? Is there something with which I may assist?"

"Not at all," said Bingley, ignoring his neighbor's humor. "As I have leased this property, it behooves me to foster good relations with you. I look on this as an excellent opportunity to do just that."

Bennet regarded Bingley as his lips curled into the hint of a smile. "Then perhaps you will ride with me for a time. There is a gate ahead where you may cross over to my property."

Agreeing between them, they made their way forward to the gate, which lay no more than a quarter of a mile distant. As they rode, Darcy regarded the man surreptitiously, trying to determine something about him, discover what sort of man he was. Mr. Bennet was a tall man, nearly as tall as Darcy, and if Darcy was not qualified to determine it for himself, he thought ladies would find him attractive. Beyond these physical attributes, Darcy decided he was an intelligent man, as he had noted during those few short moments at the assembly, a man of quickness and competence, though his sense of humor spoke of one who had experienced life's bitterness, and now found the world dark and diverting.

In a particular way, Darcy thought the man was not dissimilar to Darcy himself. Darcy too had known the virulent sting of disappointment and betrayal, had suffered loss and agony. Hunted for his wealth by more than Miss Bingley alone, Darcy had hungered for the company of those who saw him as a man and appreciated him for himself, while tolerating his weaknesses as he extended the same balm to them. It was one of the many reasons Darcy enjoyed Bingley's company so much, for there was naught of pretension about him, nothing of avarice or grasping in his friendship. Bingley's friendship was true. It was a shame his sister was not cut from the same cloth.

"Welcome to Longbourn, gentlemen," said Bennet when they reached the gate and the two men crossed over. "Tell me, was your purpose this morning pleasure, or were you engaged in some business of the estate?"

"Pleasure, to be certain," replied Bingley, flashing Bennet his customary grin. "You might say that the atmosphere at Netherfield is a little stifling."

"Is that so?" Bennet gave the impression of a man holding in his laughter by a thread. "Well, that, at least, I can understand, and likely better than you. I am a lone man in a house filled with four females and their attendant concerns. It is sometimes overwhelming."

Bingley grinned. "I only have two sisters, but I well remember the experience before Louisa married. What of you, Mr. Bennet? Have you come out today for the pleasure of the ride?"

"This morning I was called to a tenant cottage." Mr. Bennet paused and shrugged. "It was not a serious matter. I was returning to Longbourn when I came across you fine gentlemen."

For a time, they spoke of their estates as they rode, Mr. Bennet first sharing his impressions of his estate, then answering some questions Bingley had about Netherfield. The man was not a fount of knowledge, though he appeared competent. Rather, he spoke with a negligent sort of ease, as if the information he possessed was not important to him. Darcy might have expected to find a dilatory man from the way he spoke, a man who bestirred himself only when he must. Yet he could see all around them, though they were in a wilder section of the estate, appeared orderly, directed by a competent hand in a way that would have been distinct if that direction had been lacking.

"You mentioned living in a home with four ladies," said Bingley after a time of this. "As I recall, four ladies from your house attended the assembly."

"That is true," said Mr. Bennet affably. "My eldest, Jane, is the young woman with whom you danced twice."

Bingley grinned, devoid of any sense of embarrassment, a fact that seemed to divert Bennet.

"My younger daughters are Elizabeth, Mary, and Catherine, whom we call Kitty. My wife, God rest her soul, perished trying to bring a fifth daughter into the world. Had she and the child survived, I might have had to endure *six* ladies!"

Though it was not a matter about which to laugh, Darcy sensed that the man had overcome his losses, unsurprising since they had, given his youngest daughter's age, occurred more than a decade before. Bingley, it seemed, had the sense not to pursue that line of conversation, instead, choosing to alter it slightly.

"A handsome collection of ladies they are."

"Oh, aye," replied Bennet, "they are often on the tongues of those who discuss pleasant young ladies. Perhaps I ought to have judged better and remarried when I lost my companion, but I have been content in their company these many years. They have fortunes enough between them that they will not suffer should I depart this life early, but they will not live at this estate any longer."

"An entail?" asked Darcy, speaking for the first time.

"Instituted by my great grandfather," confirmed Bennet. "Had I sired a son, I would have ended it. As it is . . ."

Bennet shrugged, signifying it was a matter not worth discussing and too late, regardless. In that, Darcy agreed with him. One might wish to pass his property to his progeny—such considerations were paramount to a man in Darcy's position—but Darcy could understand the disinclination to marry again. By Mr. Bennet's testimony, he had provided for his daughters. That must be sufficient.

"That is understandable," said Bingley, voicing Darcy's thoughts. "My father was the same. After my mother's passing, he had little interest in remarrying."

"Then he left you responsible for your sisters?" asked Bennet.

Bingley nodded. "Louisa was already engaged when my father passed. But Caroline has been my responsibility."

Bennet chortled at Bingley's tight tone. "She is a handful, is she?"

"You have no notion, Mr. Bennet," replied Bingley with a grimace.

"And you, sir?" asked Bennet, turning to Darcy. "I understand you are also bereft of a father's guidance. Do you also have other siblings in your care?"

"Only one much younger sister," replied Darcy. "Georgiana is but sixteen years old. Unlike Bingley's sister, she is of a complying temperament, though she can give trouble when she wishes."

"Nonsense, Darcy!" exclaimed Bingley, even as Darcy was considering exactly to what mischief his sister was capable. "I dare say I have never seen such a sweet, well-behaved girl as your sister. If Caroline had taken her likeness and modeled her behavior after Miss Darcy, I would have been well pleased!"

Darcy's thoughts turned to the previous summer, and how he doubted Miss Bingley had ever been in danger of throwing away her family, her heritage, and her life on a rake. That was not fair to Georgiana, for she had been put upon by a man she had thought she could trust. Yet Darcy had not been blameless in that matter. It accomplished nothing to blame his sister; any anger he had felt had long burned away, regardless.

For several long moments, they exchanged accounts of their families, their connections, and certain other details of their lives. Darcy shared his connection to the Earl of Matlock reluctantly, but other than a comment that he had not known, Bennet said nothing else. He did not seem to believe it signified, which suited Darcy very well. From Bennet, Darcy learned he had no close family of his own, but that his late wife had a brother and a sister, neither of whom were of the gentle class, and that the brother was a man of trade. Had Darcy not counted Bingley as a friend, he might have wondered if this connection made Bennet a suitable acquaintance. As it was, he did not consider it, much as Bennet had paid no attention to his relations.

"Well, gentlemen," said Mr. Bennet after a time in their company, "I believe I should return home, for I am expected. I would invite you to accompany me, for I expect you wish to be known to my daughters better."

The man smirked and added: "I have a better notion. Shall you not join us for dinner?"

Bingley looked to Darcy, who attempted to inform him without words that he had no objection. "We should be happy to attend, Mr. Bennet."

"Excellent! Then I shall have my daughter send around our card. Until then, I shall bid you farewell."

As Darcy rode away with his friend, Bingley turned to him. "Mr. Bennet appears to be an excellent man, does he not?"

"Yes, Bingley. I suspect he will be a worthy acquaintance."

When her father returned from riding the estate, Elizabeth could see at once how good his mood, how playful. The reason for it became evident at once.

"Jane, my dear, I must beg your indulgence, for we are to have visitors at Longbourn."

"Of course, Papa," replied Jane. "When and who will we host?"

"The who is the party at Netherfield Park," said Mr. Bennet with a grin. "A fact which I am certain will please you immensely. As to the when, as you are the mistress of this estate at present, that is entirely your decision." Mr. Bennet flashed her a grin and added: "Though I hope you will not, out of some perverse sense of humor, make them wait long, lest you prove me a liar."

"I shall dispatch an invitation at once, Papa," said Jane.

"Excellent. I must own that I am disappointed, Jane, for I expected at least one blush of pleasure at the news."

"Oh, without a doubt!" exclaimed Elizabeth. "It is no less than a match foreordained, given what I saw at the assembly."

"It is only unfortunate that Mr. Darcy outranks Mr. Bingley," joined Mary. "For otherwise, Mr. Bingley might escort our sister to dinner!"

Provoking Jane's embarrassment was rare enough that it was a delight when they managed it. On this occasion, Jane's cheeks pinked, though she possessed enough self-possession to respond betraying no hint of her feelings.

"You forget about Mr. Hurst, Mary. As Mr. Bingley only leases his estate, Mr. Hurst, who I understand owns his, must take precedence."

"Good girl," murmured Mr. Bennet.

"You met them on the estate?" asked Elizabeth, turning back to her father.

"On the border, close to the Johnson farm," confirmed Mr. Bennet. "I stopped and talked with them for some time." He turned his gaze on Jane and winked. "I give you leave to like them as much as you wish, for I have discovered that they are excellent gentlemen. Even Mr. Darcy, despite the high connections he possesses."

"The nephew of an earl, as I recall," said Jane.

Elizabeth was unsurprised that her sister had not mentioned it, for she was not one to consider such things. What was most interesting to Elizabeth was that the truth had not made its way around the ballroom the previous evening, for by Mary's testimony, Miss Bingley had boasted of it at least once.

"In answer to your question," said Mr. Bennet, looking to Elizabeth, "I have no notion of why our excellent gossips did not divine the important news of Mr. Darcy's connections. Perhaps Miss Bingley was so busy pursuing the gentleman that she had no time to devote to crowing about her acquaintance to anyone who listened."

"Miss Bingley is not *that* bad, Papa," said Jane before Elizabeth could inform her father of what Mary had told them.

Mr. Bennet regarded his eldest for some moments, saying nothing. When he spoke, his words were gentle, yet firm.

"In fact, I suspect she is much worse, Jane. If you like her and consider her a friend, I shall not gainsay your right to choose your friends. But I would not have you taken in. Bingley himself informed me of his sister's difficult character."

"Until I see something of it," said Jane, "I shall withhold my judgment."

"That would be for the best," agreed Mr. Bennet. Then Mr. Bennet turned to Elizabeth. "As for you, Lizzy, I also give *you* leave to like Mr. Darcy. I suspect, out of the pair of them, Mr. Darcy is the man of greater understanding, though Mr. Bingley is not deficient."

"Why do you suppose I might wish for your leave?" asked Elizabeth.

"No reason," said Mr. Bennet, though his look informed her that he was not saying everything. "Allow an old man his pride in his children, Lizzy. If Mr. Darcy does not understand your worth within a few days of knowing you, he is far blinder than I expect."

Elizabeth did not think her father intended it, but that led her sisters to turn on her, and for a time, the teasing flew back and forth between them. Mr. Bennet watched the carnage, smirking at them in his inimitable way for some moments, and then he retreated to his bookroom before the ladies could band together against him.

"While I would enjoy your continued company," said he as he rose, "there are certain tasks I should complete this afternoon. Thus, I ask for your indulgence."

Before he left the room, however, he approached Elizabeth, touching her cheek, while settling a hand on Kitty's arm. "Indeed, I am proud, for no man could have better or more beautiful daughters than you all. You are all coming to the age where I might lose your hearts to other men. But I shall not repine it, knowing that is the fate *all* men must someday face. Instead, I shall keep the memories of you with me to sustain me when you all leave me."

Then with a smile, he departed. Mr. Bennet was not a sentimental man, Elizabeth knew. Thus, such times were to be cherished, for they did not happen often.

CHAPTER IV

*I*t did not surprise Darcy when Miss Bingley showed her disapproval when informed of the Bennets' invitation to dinner. What did surprise him was how Bingley essentially ignored her when she complained of his acceptance, answering when he felt necessary, but otherwise choosing the path of least resistance rather than argument. Darcy had often counseled his friend regarding his sister, for she had the wherewithal to ruin him in society. Now, the time spent in a house over which the woman presided had forced him to acknowledge she was uncontrollable, that perhaps Bingley had not misjudged his approach.

Darcy watched Miss Bingley as they sat in the carriage on the way to Longbourn on the evening in question, and he could not help but attempt to puzzle her out, though his success in understanding her was limited. It was strange that Miss Bingley, a woman who was conscious of all matters of society, could so profoundly misunderstand the responsibilities of gentlefolk when at their estates.

Regardless of the difference in situations, the relative sizes of properties, and the prominence of connections, it was incumbent on members of the gentleman class to foster good relations with their neighbors. The drawbacks of being at odds with one's neighbor could not be understated. This was as true for a man who had long held sway over his property as it was for a man leasing an estate for the first time. Miss Bingley, in her eagerness to set herself on a higher level than those who were deserving of respect, could not see it.

"I cannot understand why you accepted this invitation," complained Miss Bingley as the carriage progressed through the deepening gloom of the coming evening. It was not yet dark, but Darcy thought night would fall before they sat down to dinner. "Is it not enough that we must endure these people in what this community calls society? I should prefer to remain at Netherfield with our family party."

"Mr. Bennet invited us, and I agreed we will attend," replied Bingley, his tone suggesting he was not listening to his sister. "I will not offend my new neighbor by refusing."

"It would be better if you had," muttered the woman. "Then we would be free of their attempts to claim an acquaintance with us."

That the acquaintance was already in place did not bear mentioning — Miss Bingley already understood this, regardless of her wish it was not. What most annoyed Darcy was the suggestion that those in the neighborhood attempted to draw close to the Bingleys for societal benefit — as if the Bingleys were an old noble family and not the scions of a tradesman in the process of becoming landed. While she might suggest there was a reason for others to covet a connection with them, considering their wealth and the relative lack of those who lived nearby, Darcy had seen nothing of it. There were always those who were alert for any opportunity to improve their lot; the Bennets were not of their ilk.

Such complaints continued the entire drive to Longbourn, and Darcy was not the only member of the company fatigued by the sound of her voice. The Bennets were beneath them; it was a mistake to give them such consequence; they should take care for those artful Bennet girls, for who knew of what they were capable in their lust to make matches with wealthy men. By the time they sighted Longbourn church through the trees, the woman had disgusted Darcy enough to deliver a reprimand if only to silence her. It was fortunate, therefore, that Bingley took the matter upon himself.

"That is enough, Caroline," said he when his sister took a breath to continue her harangue.

Darcy could not see her well in the gloom of the carriage, but he thought her look at her brother was no less than poisonous.

"Have done. We are almost at Longbourn, and I will not have you insulting our neighbors. If you can say nothing civil, then it would be better if you said nothing, for that will offend our hosts less."

"Do you suppose I cannot behave properly?" demanded Miss Bingley with some heat.

"Given what I am seeing before me," retorted Bingley, "there is some question of whether you can."

"Perhaps you should question whether those Bennet girls know how to behave," sniffed Miss Bingley with contempt. "You need not worry about me, Brother, for I am well acquainted with all the social graces."

Darcy was unable to keep his own counsel. "You decry acquaintance with a gentle family, one which is long established at their property. It is unseemly to disdain such friendships, Miss Bingley, especially as they are your brother's neighbors."

"Of course, Mr. Darcy," simpered Miss Bingley. "It is only my low tolerance for poor behavior that motivates my disquiet. I shall behave with perfect propriety, regardless of distaste for their poor behavior."

It was not worthwhile to respond. Darcy thought his friend threw him a grateful glance, but as the carriage halted before the doors of Longbourn, there was no further opportunity to respond.

Within moments of their guests arriving, Elizabeth had taken the likeness of each, her observations confirming her previous opinions. Mr. Bingley was effusive, charming, and eager, and as he showed those qualities toward Elizabeth's eldest sister, she found herself contented. Mrs. Hurst was quiet, often speaking only in a soft voice, and while she was not objectionable, Elizabeth did not feel like she had much in common with the elder of Mr. Bingley's sisters. By contrast, the lady's husband was nothing less than a bore, speaking in grunts and reserving his attention for the plate of sweetmeats Jane had provided for their guests' enjoyment.

Of the remaining two, Mr. Darcy remained reserved, though he spoke with her father with no hint of reluctance or misplaced pride. When he spoke, Elizabeth had the impression, much as she had at the assembly, that the man was intelligent, that he did not speak unless he knew something of the subject at hand.

It was unfortunate, but that evening confirmed the impression Elizabeth had gained of Miss Bingley in every particular. She did not care for the Bennets—she made that clear with every sneer, every clipped response she made to anyone who dared speak to her. Her excessive opinion of her worth did not bear consideration, nor did any obvious comparisons between her situation in life and the Bennets'. Thus, Elizabeth decided it was best to turn her attention to other matters and avoid the source of discord in the room. That was easier to do in word than deed.

"How are you finding Netherfield, Bingley?" asked Elizabeth's father when they gathered in the sitting-room awaiting the call to dinner. "Has the estate met your expectations?"

"In every particular, Mr. Bennet," said Mr. Bingley, showing his ever-present grin and ignoring his sister's disdainful huff.

"Then you are ready to declare your undying devotion to our small community and stay forever?"

It was clear from Mr. Bingley's answering grin he understood the jest in Mr. Bennet's statement. Miss Bingley, however, was not so discerning.

"You have my apologies, Mr. Bennet," said she, her rank insincerity wafting through the room, "but Hertfordshire is not sufficient for my family's needs."

"Is that so, Miss Bingley?" asked Mr. Bennet, diverted by her pride. "Then I suppose you must mean more than Netherfield's suitability, for though estates present unique challenges, one is not that much different from the next."

"It must be as you say. But I, for one, require more from society than what Hertfordshire can offer."

"Dare I ask where you might find a suitable location?" asked Elizabeth, unable to help herself. "Would you prefer Cornwall? Or perhaps Cheshire is more to your taste?"

"Cornwall is, indeed, too far from London for my taste," said Miss Bingley with a sniff of disdain. "I think I might prefer my brother to settle in the north, for the country there is much more pleasing than it is here."

"But Caroline," said Mr. Bingley, "unless I am mistaken, I believe Cornwall is no further distant than Derbyshire, for example. Moreover, Cornwall's climate must be preferable to the north where it can become rather cold."

It was clear to everyone present that Mr. Bingley's mention of Derbyshire was not accidental. Kitty giggled into her hand though Mary prevented further outburst with a sharp look at her sister. Miss Bingley understood it better than anyone else if her glare at her brother was any indication. She did not deign to respond.

"England is not large," said Mr. Darcy into the sudden mixture of tension and mirth. "Derbyshire is not *that* far north of London, after all. We do get more snow, but it does not become much colder."

"Aye, that is true, Darcy," said Mr. Bennet. "Then I suppose the climate is not enough to provoke you to sell your estate and relocate to warmer climes."

"Sell Pemberley!" demanded Miss Bingley before Mr. Darcy could respond. "If you had ever seen that grand estate, Mr. Bennet, you would never suggest such a thing. It is unthinkable!"

Mr. Bennet listened to Miss Bingley's outrage and turned a grin and an arched eyebrow on Mr. Darcy. The gentleman did not hesitate to accept the challenge.

"Miss Bingley is correct, Mr. Bennet. I would not relinquish Pemberley for any sum of money. My family has called it home for centuries."

"Then we think alike, Darcy," said Mr. Bennet. Though his grin never faded, Elizabeth could hear the pointed nature of his words, though he did not look back at Miss Bingley. "Longbourn has been in my family for generations. Though I dare say it is not nearly so large or prosperous as Pemberley, we are fond of it, nonetheless."

"Are you attempting to compare this place with Pemberley?" demanded Miss Bingley.

"If you recall what I said, you know I am not," said Mr. Bennet, his tone mild. "My only point was that pride in one's heritage, the works of one's hands is not solely the province of those blessed with great wealth or a lofty position in society."

Miss Bingley's sniff of disdain informed them of her opinion. "Then it appears you have failed, Mr. Bennet. Or are the rumors of an entail on your estate false?"

"No, they are true enough, Miss Bingley," said Mr. Bennet with good humor. "Your comments about my failure I shall ignore and remind you that no one can control such things as the sex of one's offspring.

"My heir may not share my surname, but he is of my blood, meaning my family's stewardship over the property will continue."

Miss Bingley might have responded, but at that moment two things forestalled her. The first was the clearing of her brother's throat, while the second was the entrance of the housekeeper announcing dinner. As if wishing to end the discomfort and antagonistic nature of the conversation, Mr. Bennet rose and offered his arm to Mrs. Hurst, who accepted it with obvious relief. Mr. Darcy rose to offer his arm to Jane, and the other two gentlemen each escorted two ladies into the dining room.

The dinner partners were not precisely pleased with each other. Her father, she noted, spoke with Mrs. Hurst in an easy, if banal fashion, while Mr. Darcy, she suspected, was the same with Jane. Mr. Hurst concentrated on his dinner to the exclusion of all other concerns, while Miss Bingley nursed her annoyance in silence, looking about as if she did not appreciate her position in the middle of the table. The daughter of a tradesman and unmarried, she was the lowest-ranked of the company, regardless of her disinclination to acknowledge that truth.

"It must have been difficult," said Mrs. Hurst to Mr. Bennet after a time. "Your wife passed many years ago as I understand."

"She did," said Mr. Bennet. "But she gave me four lovely daughters who have done me proud."

"What of the need to uphold your position in society?" asked Miss Bingley. "Your daughters must have been very young when you lost your wife."

"They were," confirmed Mr. Bennet. "But I am not of a social disposition, Miss Bingley."

"It matters not if you appreciate society. What matters is for any family to maintain its position, they must be active participants."

"Perhaps that is true," said Mr. Bennet with a shrug. "While my daughters were too young, I upheld the family's honor by attending where I could. When Jane reached the appropriate age, we again hosted our neighbors. I dare say our reputation and position did not suffer in the intervening years."

While Miss Bingley did not agree, for once she held her tongue and did not respond further. Elizabeth, who sat near her father, listened as he turned his attention back to Mrs. Hurst, and if their conversation was not precisely interesting, at least it was civil. For the rest of the meal, Miss Bingley said little, which appeared to suit them all. After the meal, the gentlemen lingered in the dining room with their port for only a few moments before they joined the ladies in the sitting-room. While Mr. Bingley went to Jane at once and Mr. Hurst to his wife, who had situated her sister near her side, no doubt to prevent further outbursts, Elizabeth was interested to note that Mr. Darcy chose to approach her.

"Thank you, Miss Elizabeth, for this excellent evening. My compliments to your cook—she clearly knows her business."

"Aye, we are the envy of the district for her loyalty," replied Elizabeth. "But then, I assume, being a man who can afford it, you must also employ excellent cooks."

"I do," said Mr. Darcy. "But I can recognize greatness when it confronts me."

Elizabeth laughed at his turn of phrase. "I shall pass your praise on to her, though I suspect the term 'greatness' will prompt her to think entirely too well of herself."

Mr. Darcy chuckled along with her. "This evening has been enjoyable, Miss Elizabeth. Does your sister manage the house herself, or do you all assist her?"

"We all have some hand in it," replied Elizabeth, "though Jane has the final decision. At present we are attempting to teach Kitty what must be done, for she is coming to the age where she must know such things."

"That is prudent," said Mr. Darcy, nodding. "It is well that Miss Bennet has the reins, for it has often been said that too many cooks spoil the broth."

"That is true," said Elizabeth. "But what of you, sir? As I recall, you have also been without a mistress in your house for many years, since before you were the master of your estate."

"You have the right of it," said Mr. Darcy. "Like your father, I am not a social man, and my father was less than even I. Georgiana, my sister, is now sixteen, and while she is not out, we may host small gatherings. She is of a retiring temperament and is yet uncertain of herself. Once I marry, perhaps I shall entertain more."

"Then has your position in society suffered as a result?"

Mr. Darcy laughed at her arch question. "No, I do not believe it has. Were I able to host and declined to do it, I suspect others would wonder. At present I am content."

"Ah, then there is some hope for we who are not prominent in society." Mr. Darcy did not miss Elizabeth's glance at Miss Bingley, who appeared annoyed that they were together, but remained with her sister. "For if you, who are accounted as a man high in society, may withstand your absence, then perhaps we, who are coarse and unpolished may also survive in a society that is so confined and unvarying."

"I dare say it will be well."

The gentleman's comment was absent, Elizabeth thought, for he regarded her for a long moment. What he might be thinking, Elizabeth could not say, for he was closed to her, unreadable as a stone wall.

"You have my apologies, Miss Elizabeth, but I believe I understand your turn of phrase. Might I assume you overheard my comment to Miss Bingley the evening of the assembly?"

For a moment, Elizabeth did not understand him. Then she recalled the second time she had overheard them that evening and realized she had echoed his comments, although unconsciously. Uncertain what she should say, Elizabeth floundered, a sensation that was not at all familiar to her.

"I can see you did," said Mr. Darcy while Elizabeth was trying to gather her wits. "I hope you understand that I meant no offense."

"Oh," asked Elizabeth, finding her voice in response to his denial. "As I recall, I could think of several interpretations of what you said. Do you care to inform me which you meant?"

Mr. Darcy chuckled and shook his head. "You are entirely too quick, Miss Elizabeth. I cannot attempt to obfuscate, for you will see through me without difficulty."

"Are you inclined to do so?"

"Not at all," said the gentleman at once, his exaggerated response a show of fear for her displeasure. "But I had best take care, for if I do not, you will let me know of my failings, I suspect.

"In answer to your question," continued he, "my comment to Miss Bingley was no more and no less than you might think. It has been my experience that small societies are much the same wherever one goes. In many ways, I find those who inhabit them to be far more genuine and estimable than those of higher society, who feel restraint does not apply to them."

"As I recall, you used the word 'coarse.'"

"That I did, but only in response to Miss Bingley," said Mr. Darcy. "What some call coarse, others might term unpretentious."

"The question is whether you do."

"It depends on the person and the situation." Mr. Darcy smiled. "In this instance, I would not call your neighbors indelicate, though I would also not call their manners fashionable. As I do not appreciate fashionable manners that is not necessarily a criticism."

"Then we shall speak no more on the subject," said Elizabeth, relieved she had been correct.

Leaving the subject behind, they became easier with each other, their conversation devolving to other, less fraught concerns, but which were of interest to them both. At times, Elizabeth thought their conversation became animated, for they spoke of matters of which their opinions were not alike, and they both defended their positions vigorously. Elizabeth had so rarely engaged in debate, other than with her father or aunt and uncle, that she found she enjoyed the exchange of ideas, the back and forth of parry and riposte, of making your argument before a determined foe.

It was no surprise to Elizabeth after the fact that it was impossible that certain others would allow them to continue in this manner. That they had gone on as long as they had was curious, for the interests of certain others in the group were such that any interaction between them must be anathema. However it happened, at length, Miss Bingley shrugged off whatever bands her sister had cast over her and rose to approach them. To Mr. Darcy, she gave an expression she must have calculated as beguiling, but the fire of her gaze whenever her eyes found Elizabeth told the truth of her anger.

"Mr. Darcy!" exclaimed the woman. "How good of you to give Miss Elizabeth your attention."

"Not at all, Miss Bingley," replied Darcy. "I have enjoyed our conversation very much."

"I suppose everyone can have something intelligent to say at one time or another."

Mr. Darcy's countenance darkened at the insult, but Elizabeth could scarcely hold in her laughter. It seemed the gentleman realized this, for he did not unleash the retort Elizabeth was certain he had poised on the tip of his tongue.

"May I ask what you were speaking?" said Miss Bingley, sitting nearby. "Perhaps I may add something to it."

"Oh no, that will not do," said Elizabeth, holding in her mirth. "I shall cede Mr. Darcy's company to you, Miss Bingley, for I believe you have much of which to speak."

Elizabeth meant to convey humor and a desire to avoid further unpleasantness. Mr. Darcy's plaintive look almost cracked her composure, but that was nothing compared to Miss Bingley's smugness. That Mr. Darcy did not care for her company was a matter she did not seem capable of grasping. Elizabeth did not concern herself with that, however, choosing to excuse herself to go to her father's side.

"I am surprised at you, Lizzy," said her father in a low tone when she drew near. "I might not have thought Miss Bingley had the resources to send you fleeing."

"You would not be incorrect, Papa," said Elizabeth. "Given her general demeanor, discretion seems the best option."

Mr. Bennet chuckled. "The sight of Darcy squirming under her tender ministrations provides its own rewards."

A glance at Mr. Darcy confirmed Mr. Bennet's observation. While it was not laudable to enjoy the gentleman's discomfort, Elizabeth resolved to ignore it for the moment. The gentleman had earned it with his words, though he had, she supposed, redeemed himself with his explanation. The next time they were in company, she would consider the matter better and push back against Miss Bingley's designs. It was not *her* responsibility to protect the gentleman from her depredations.

Later, after their guests departed, Elizabeth sat in her bedroom, her eyes fixed on the fire, the memories of the evening playing out in the dancing figures of the crackling flames. What she thought of Mr. Darcy she could not quite say, though the thought he was an estimable gentleman was near the top of her thoughts. When the knock on her door startled her, she realized she had sat motionless for longer than she had any notion.

Jane entered when Elizabeth called out, and Elizabeth could see something troubled her sister at once. Elizabeth beckoned to her sister, asking: "What is it, Jane."

While Jane remained silent for a moment, at length she sighed and gave Elizabeth a crooked smile. "It appears you were correct, Lizzy. Miss Bingley was no less than insolent tonight. It appears she cares nothing for us."

Elizabeth sighed and gave her sister a nod. "It is unfortunate, Jane, but it was obvious from the moment we met."

"Is it not best to give others the benefit of our assumption of their goodness?"

Reaching out to clasp Jane's hand, she squeezed and said: "It is, Jane, and I am convinced you are the best of us because of it. I understand you are not deficient, and that I am much more apt to think the worst of others. The knowledge that I am correct gives me no pleasure."

That seemed to bring Jane some relief, for she smiled and settled back onto Elizabeth's bed. "But we shall not meet incivility with the same. Miss Bingley may think what she wishes. We Bennets will not abandon our good manners."

"Of course not, Jane. Perish the thought."

The sisters regarded each other for a long moment and then burst into laughter. They remained together late into the night, enjoying each other's company as they had many times throughout the years.

CHAPTER V

*D*inner with the Netherfield party broke any barrier that might have existed between the two families, other than the obvious, of course. As Miss Bingley did not appreciate anyone in the district, they felt themselves equal to the task of ignoring her. Had she known that Mr. Bingley was universally admired while she was universally considered haughty and above her company, perhaps Miss Bingley might have moderated her behavior. Then again, it was more than likely she would not care in the slightest. Regardless, most of those in the neighborhood spoke to her only when they must, avoiding the rough side of her tongue, and to this, Miss Bingley seemed perfectly indifferent.

Of more importance to the gossips was the sight of what occurred between the Netherfield party and those at Longbourn. While events of the neighborhood were not exactly plentiful, there were enough that it was quickly growing apparent that Mr. Bingley preferred the company of Longbourn's eldest daughter, while Mr. Darcy was drawn to the second daughter. It was not long before rumors arose of imminent proposals.

What Mr. Darcy and Mr. Bingley thought of these rumors Elizabeth could not say; to the best of her knowledge, they did not know how often their names were on the tongues of the gossips. Their newer introduction to the society of the area rendered them less certain of intimacy, and less likely to be included in the tittle-tattle arising about them. That the gossip also centered on them shielded them from any knowledge of it.

For Elizabeth's part, she was pleased with the gentlemen's actions, considered Mr. Bingley to be an excellent match for Jane, and appreciated Mr. Darcy's intelligence and calm, stolid demeanor. Whether he would eventually pay her the ultimate compliment Elizabeth could not say. What she did know was that she was enjoying the opportunity to come to know him better, to learn more of the enigmatic gentleman, who was quickly becoming the most interesting man she had ever known.

Miss Bingley, by contrast, appeared to ignore the implications of Mr. Darcy's actions toward Elizabeth, even as she was certain the woman schemed to pull her brother from his admiration of Jane. That did not mean she remained sanguine when Mr. Darcy turned his attention on Elizabeth. Many a time the woman sought to interpose herself between them, drawing Mr. Darcy's attention to herself and sneering at Elizabeth. Invariably when Miss Bingley stuck her long nose between them, Elizabeth would allow it, turning with good humor to other friends, watching with amusement as Mr. Darcy would don his patient demeanor and endure the woman as best he could.

"I must own to feeling rather ill-used, Miss Elizabeth," said Mr. Darcy on one occasion during a dinner they both attended and after he had escaped from the woman's prowling. "This is the third time you have abandoned me to Miss Bingley's mercy with nary a thought for my feelings on the subject."

Elizabeth regarded him, feeling hilarity well up within her breast. "Do you suppose I should call Miss Bingley out for her temerity? Pistols at dawn?"

"Perhaps that would be precipitous," replied the gentleman. Elizabeth could well see the merriment in his eyes. "But you could at least stay when she comes and protect me from her."

At that, Elizabeth could not help but laugh. "I never thought I would see the day that a big, strong man such as you could not defend yourself against a woman."

"She is not a woman," confided Darcy. "She is a succubus, determined to seduce me and spirit me away to her fiery realm of agony and despair."

Elizabeth only laughed harder, Mr. Darcy joining in. On the far side

of the room, she caught sight of Miss Bingley sitting next to her sister —
if she was not accosting Mr. Darcy, Miss Bingley was always next to
Mrs. Hurst. The way she watched them, Elizabeth could imagine the
molten lava the woman might have conjured over her head had she
only possessed the power. Not wishing to give her the impression that
she was watching, Elizabeth kept her attention on Mr. Darcy.

"Then perhaps you should employ a priest to exorcize her attempts
to damn you."

"Yes, that might be for the best," said Mr. Darcy, still chuckling.

Turning, the man watched as several of the younger members of
the company flocked toward where Mary was playing the pianoforte,
entreating her to play a song so they might dance. It was not
uncommon at gatherings such as this — and at Sir William's parties in
particular — that there might be dancing. Kitty and Maria Lucas led this
effort, as young ladies not yet out and not having as many
opportunities to take part in the amusement. Mary, though she was
fond of performing, was not averse to providing for their enjoyment,
and began playing a lively tune.

"I see the young ladies are eager to dance," observed Mr. Darcy.

"As they usually are," replied Elizabeth. "It happens often."

"Then perhaps you would like to join them?" asked Mr. Darcy. "I
should be happy to dance with you if you are of a mind."

Flattered, Elizabeth agreed, and soon she found herself on the edge
of the line, dancing around Mr. Darcy. While this was a livelier and
less formal dance than that they had shared at the assembly, Mr. Darcy
proved himself as adept as he had that evening, and Elizabeth enjoyed
their exertions immensely.

"Well, Lizzy," said Charlotte later when she had separated from the
gentleman. "I can see this fascination between you and Mr. Darcy
continues apace."

The gentleman, Elizabeth noted, had escaped Miss Bingley by
taking himself to Mr. Bennet's side, where the two were now engaged
in quiet conversation. The woman examined him with longing in her
eyes, but she stayed by her sister for the moment, watchful for the right
moment to pounce.

"He is an excellent gentleman, Charlotte. But there is nothing
imminent between us."

"No, I dare say there is not," replied Charlotte. "But there could be
with very little effort on your part. I certainly would never have
expected to see Mr. Darcy dancing in a company such as this."

"Nor would I," murmured Elizabeth.

"I wish you the best, my friend," said Charlotte, drawing Elizabeth into an embrace. "I know you have always wished for a marriage of mutual respect and love; from what I am seeing before me, I suspect you might just find it."

Blushing crimson, Elizabeth turned back to her friend and gave her a shy nod, to which Charlotte smiled and grasped her shoulder. Then she moved away, releasing Elizabeth to an earnest contemplation of the gentleman. While she had not misunderstood Mr. Darcy's preference for her company, Elizabeth had given little serious thought to the gentleman's motivations. Now, for the first time, she considered what might be, what her future might hold. Could she love Mr. Darcy? She thought the answer was obvious, though she had not reached that lofty state. But it was possible, and it was coming tantalizingly closer with each passing day.

A little later that evening, Elizabeth happened to overhear a conversation that raised her hopes ever higher. Speaking with a friend, she had not noticed as she drifted closer to where Mr. Darcy was standing with a gentleman of the neighborhood. When the man departed, Miss Bingley, who had seemingly lain in wait, took the opportunity to accost him.

"Mr. Darcy!" exclaimed she in a voice that others could overhear. "What an excellent gentleman you are, giving your consequence to these people, though I fancy I understand something of your true feelings."

Had Mr. Darcy ground his teeth in frustration, Elizabeth fancied she might have heard it through the din of conversation. "No, Miss Bingley, I am completely at ease. It is an excellent evening."

"Oh, you need say no more, for I understand you perfectly." Out of the corner of her eye, Elizabeth could see the woman regarding the gentleman with some suspicion. "I *have* noticed that you reserve a significant measure of your attention for Miss Elizabeth Bennet. It is a curious choice, for she possesses little in the way of admirable qualities."

This appeared too much for Mr. Darcy, for though he was facing away from her, Elizabeth could readily see the sudden stiffness in his back. "Miss Elizabeth is one of the most admirable ladies of my acquaintance, Miss Bingley. She is an excellent woman, can hold her own in any debate, and possesses some of the finest eyes I have ever seen. From the first moment of our acquaintance, I have considered her among the best of women."

Then Mr. Darcy gave her a perfunctory bow and stalked away,

leaving Miss Bingley watching him. Then she turned a poisonous glare on Elizabeth, who was studiously looking away and marched across the room to her sister again.

"It appears you have made an enemy, Lizzy," said Penelope Long, who had missed no more of the conversation than Elizabeth had herself.

"Miss Bingley is an enemy to us all," retorted Elizabeth.

"That much is clear," replied Penelope. "But I am far more interested in Mr. Darcy's apparent admiration for you. I might never have expected one of our local ladies to catch such a prominent gentleman. Then again, I suppose I should have expected it of *you*."

Elizabeth gave her friend a weak grin. "There is nothing between us, Penelope."

"Something is growing, despite your protests." Penelope grasped Elizabeth's arm and squeezed. "Thank you, my friend, for you have given me hope. If you can catch the eye of such a gentleman, I must believe that I may be similarly blessed."

Then Penelope departed, leaving Elizabeth to her thoughts. And pleasant thoughts they were, dominated by a chivalrous and handsome knight, and the castle he might gift to his beloved bride. Yes, they were pleasant thoughts, indeed.

Darcy knew he had made a tactical error when he had spoken to Miss Bingley of Miss Elizabeth's virtues. Had he any concern for Miss Elizabeth's hardiness in the face of the other woman's attacks, he might have regretted it. Yet, he knew she was proof against anything Miss Bingley might try. No, Darcy was far more vulnerable by far to Miss Bingley's intrigues, for he knew from the woman's own admission that she meant to have him for a husband whatever the cost. Thus, it befitted Darcy to take care whenever he was in her company, for he would not countenance her ensnaring him.

That did not stop the woman from doing her utmost to turn his attention to her whenever she had the chance. Darcy could endure such things. What he could not endure was the thought of being tied to a bitter shrew for the rest of his life. That, he must avoid at all costs.

It was fortunate that Longbourn provided such a ready retreat from the discomfort of her attentions. Miss Bingley, now aware of his growing admiration for Miss Elizabeth, often accompanied them to the estate so she could watch for herself, interrupting whenever she felt particularly threatened. On many mornings, however, he went out riding with Bingley, and often on such occasions, they found their way to Longbourn. Miss Bingley never suspected their activities, and neither Bingley nor Darcy saw fit to illuminate her understanding. On one such occasion, Darcy heard a bit of news that astonished him exceedingly.

"You have been much at my house of late, gentleman," observed Bennet that morning as Darcy and Bingley were visiting the family in the Bennets' sitting-room.

"I hope you do not wish for our absence," was Bingley's grinning reply. "That would be a genuine tragedy, for I believe Darcy will agree with me in apprehending that the company at Longbourn is far superior to that at Netherfield."

"That *is* a surprise, Bingley," chortled Bennet. "For those at Netherfield are your sisters and your brother-in-law."

"And yet, I shall not recant," said Bingley. Then he turned his lazy gaze on Darcy and said: "You agree with me, do you not?"

"Without hesitation," replied Darcy, gazing deeply into Miss Elizabeth's fathomless eyes.

He noted her cheeks lighting up in a dusty hue, even as she returned his scrutiny. That she was not averse to his presence had been clear from the start. This was perhaps the first sign he had of her true feelings. It was promising, as were his burgeoning feelings for her.

"Then I regret to inform you that our company shall receive an addition early next week, and I fear it shall not be as welcome."

"Oh, Papa," said Miss Elizabeth, breaking the spell she had cast over him. "You have never even met Mr. Collins. How can you say he will be objectionable?"

"Please allow me the discernment to read between the lines," replied Bennet. "His ridiculous nature is written in every word of his correspondence. I anticipate the diversion keenly. Besides, I knew Mr. Collins's father, and while he was more objectionable than diverting, he was not devoid of folly himself."

"This Mr. Collins is a relation?" asked Darcy.

"My heir," replied Bennet. "While I do not recall the exact relation between us, I believe he is a third or fourth cousin. He is also the only living heir under the terms of the entail."

"You believe he will be objectionable?" asked Bingley.

"Silly rather than objectionable," said Bennet. "I shall savor the delights of his folly, but I expect he will exhaust my amusement and try my patience long before he leaves. My daughters, I have no doubt, will wish to avoid him as much as they can."

"You mentioned you have never made his acquaintance?" asked

Darcy.

"There was a longstanding disagreement between his father and me. We parted ways before his son was born." Bennet paused and shrugged. "But the man is my heir, and as he has offered an olive branch, I do not think it is prudent to shun him."

Darcy nodded. "Yes, that is likely for the best."

"I am not anticipating his coming," said Miss Catherine, a theatrical shudder accompanying her words. "He sounds like a rank dullard."

While it might be said the girl had spoken out of turn, Darcy could not fault her.

"Does this Mr. Collins come from a great distance?" asked Darcy.

"Kent," replied his new friend. "It seems he has recently received his ordination and has had the extraordinarily good fortune to come to the notice of the mistress of a grand estate near Westerham. That, as much as anything else, appears to have given him an inflated opinion of his worth."

A premonition wormed its way into Darcy's consciousness. His mind returned to a conversation with his uncle, where the earl had informed him of his aunt's new parson at Rosings Park. At one time, Darcy had visited his aunt's estate every spring to assist her with the books and the management of the property, but since his cousin's death two years earlier, Lady Catherine had preferred her brother's company to her nephew's. No doubt, that was due to the loss of her dream to marry Darcy to her only daughter.

"Did your cousin perchance mention the name of his patroness?" asked Darcy.

Bennet regarded him with no little curiosity. "A Lady Catherine de Bourgh, as I recall."

Darcy nodded, wondering at the chance that led his aunt's parson to an estate nearby. "Then I believe I can confirm your apprehension concerning your upcoming visitor."

"You know something of Mr. Collins?" asked Bennet, his eyebrow raising in his surprise.

"Of Mr. Collins, no," replied Darcy. "But his patroness is my aunt and knowing of her preferences in those who serve her, I suspect he is ridiculous or craven."

Bennet chortled. "That is truly a curious coincidence, Darcy. I shall be sure to introduce you to my cousin during his stay so you may learn if your conjecture is correct."

The notion of subjecting himself to one of Lady Catherine's lackeys was not palatable, but Darcy agreed readily enough. In all honesty, he could own to a little curiosity regarding this Mr. Collins. The man's predecessor, a Mr. Chambers, had been the second sort of man his aunt preferred, unwilling to arise in the morning without Lady Catherine's explicit instructions that he do so. The Bennet cousin was likely the other kind, and while he might be amusing, Darcy was certain any mirth he derived from the man's behavior would soon give way to vexation.

"But why do you suppose Mr. Collins means to visit now?" asked Miss Elizabeth of Darcy some moments later when they were speaking together. "My father has spoken of his cousin and how little they each regarded the other. The man must have reared his son with tales of my father's despicable character."

"Perhaps he is not of the same ilk as his father," was Darcy's reasonable reply. "Or perhaps he has decided the breach has persisted long enough. My aunt is outspoken in her opinion that families should be united. I suspect she may have encouraged him in this matter."

Miss Elizabeth nodded and turned her attention to other subjects. For Darcy's part, he was considering Lady Catherine and his knowledge of her. While he had told Miss Elizabeth the truth, he had not offered information she did not request. Among her ladyship's frequently offered opinions were the notion that an unmarried man was a menace to society. She no doubt felt clergymen had best precede their parishioners and show them the way. Mr. Collins had obviously spoken of his cousin and his daughters; Lady Catherine would see the perfect opportunity to ensure her parson married while providing for one — and potentially all — of Bennet's daughters.

Darcy did not wish to voice this speculation aloud. It may not be true, and he preferred not to predispose the ladies against their cousin any more than their father already had. Besides, Darcy had ample proof that Bennet loved his daughters and wished the best for them. That would include protecting them from the likes of an overeager suitor, even if the man would inherit their home when Bennet was gone.

When they returned to Netherfield for luncheon, the sight of an unhappy Miss Bingley greeted them. Then again, Darcy had rarely seen the woman in any other attitude than vexation or plotting, so it did not surprise him. Her annoyance was, of course, because of their absence that morning, and the frequent forays among the local society.

There was little enough Miss Bingley said that Darcy had not heard before, so he felt all the justification of ignoring her invective, his inattention rendering her voice akin to the annoying buzzing of a gnat. Instead, he was contemplating Miss Elizabeth, trying to determine how deep his feelings for her now went, planning what he would do if this Mr. Collins fixed his attentions on her. If the man was anything like he expected, it might tempt him to request Bingley hold him down while Darcy administered retribution for even considering himself good enough to woo her.

Through the day it went, and after a time in Miss Bingley's company, Darcy felt fatigued, such that he wished to depart from her company. However, he was a man raised to observe all matters of propriety and attending his hostess was part of that. Thus, it was late that evening, after the ladies had retired, before he was blissfully out of her presence.

"Can I assume you were at Longbourn again today?" asked Hurst the moment they reached Bingley's study, their glasses of port in hand.

"We were," confirmed Bingley. "There is no better place to while away a morning, I should think."

Hurst snorted, but his outburst carried no disdain. "Yes, we have all seen the signs of your infatuation for Miss Bennet, Bingley. I suspect your fascination will last another two or three weeks, then it will wane. Or has it already started?"

It was an unfair observation, Darcy thought, for Bingley was not *that* bad, though he had often found himself infatuated with new and pretty acquaintances. Bingley, however, did not take offense, leading Darcy to believe this was an old and worn jest between them.

"This time, I do not think it is infatuation, Hurst. Miss Bennet is unlike any other young woman I have ever met. I think I might happily fall in love with her."

The way Hurst eyed Bingley, Darcy could not say how he reacted to such news. "You will perhaps be happy. But you know how your sister will respond."

"If you will forgive me, Hurst, I care little for Caroline's opinion. Unless I was married to one of her haughty and titled friends, she would not care for my bride."

"There is some truth to that," said Hurst with a snort. "You may, of course, act as you please. My only concern is to warn you that Caroline will not take kindly to your attentions to a lady she considers unsuitable."

"And yet I am unmoved," said Bingley.

Hurst's eyes swung to Darcy, who demurred. "I have less concern for your sister's opinion, Hurst. If I decide I wish to make Miss

Elizabeth my wife, Miss Bingley's displeasure will not cause a single moment's hesitation."

"Again, I cannot fault you," said Hurst. "Caroline will not like her brother's engagement to a woman she does not choose herself, but she will endure it if she must. If she believes *you* are slipping through her grasp, I shudder to think what foolishness she might consider."

Darcy leaned forward and fixed the other man with a demanding glare. "Has she said something to give you pause?"

"This *is* Caroline of whom we are speaking, Darcy," replied Hurst with a chuckle. "She says something that concerns me so many times every day that I lose count. I have no notion of any particular scheme. But if you attempt to attach yourself to someone else, you would be foolish to assume she will not try something."

It matched Darcy's understanding of the woman, prompting his curt nod.

"Then I shall take care. I will note, however, that I have never given Miss Bingley *any* reason to hope I would offer for her."

"In Caroline's case," replied Bingley, "she does not need it. Caroline is capable of seeing what she wishes when she is of a mind. That you are my friend has been enough for her to expect a proposal these past three years."

"Three?" asked Darcy, puzzled. "It has not been two since I made her acquaintance."

"That is true," agreed Bingley. "But she had heard of you and began dreaming of being your wife long before I introduced you. Of course, she did not fix her hopes on *you*, but on the imagined delights of wealth, society, and standing she thought would be hers."

Darcy winced. "It may be best if you did not speak of your sister in such a way, Bingley."

"Perhaps it would be," said Bingley. "But you will forgive me if I do not repent of my words. Caroline has been a millstone around my neck ever since my father passed. I would give much to be free of her."

"As long as you do not think I will bring your independence to fruition."

Bingley laughed and shook his head. "No, my friend. Even if we had never spoken of the subject, I would have known you were not interested in her."

"Then I suppose we must both proceed with caution. But a time will come when she must acknowledge what she does not wish to. It may not come with the Bennet sisters but come it will, nonetheless."

With a nod, Bingley returned to his thoughts, allowing Darcy to do likewise. For the rest of their time that evening, Darcy considered the situation and Miss Bingley. Above all, he was lost in the recollection of Miss Elizabeth's perfections. Now there was a subject a man could consider for days on end and never become fatigued.

CHAPTER VI

$\mathcal{P}$erception was a blessing or a curse, depending on the situation. It was certainly no evil to possess the ability to think critically, understand events as they happened, or anticipate certain outcomes. It could often be a trial, for understanding patterns before they occurred often demanded action when one would prefer to remain aloof. Or when one preferred to avoid dealing with a fool.

When Bennet considered the matter, it was no surprise that his foolish cousin had been the means of drawing him from his comfort. The man was everything he had expected — foolishness upon silliness, a complete misunderstanding of propriety on top of an ability to give offense with no comprehension of having done so. Had Bennet set out to create a ridiculous character to fuel his diversion, he could scarcely have imagined a sillier man than William Collins. Had that been all, Bennet would have been content. It was his discernment of his cousin's motives that caused his disquiet.

"My dear cousins!" Mr. Collins had exclaimed the moment he alighted from his hired gig, his manner a mixture of excitement and pompous servility. "How fortunate I am to be in your company again. I cannot thank you enough for this opportunity to come to know you after all that has passed between us."

Bennet rejected any thought of pointing out how they had never met and that nothing had ever passed between them as too obvious and nodded to his silly cousin.

"Mr. Collins," said he, schooling his features to polite interest, "please be welcome among us. I hope your journey was not too difficult."

"Not at all," said Mr. Collins. "I spent the time considering what I might say to you, for as you know, a well-prepared mind cannot go amiss."

This time Bennet had difficulty holding his countenance, for while he was aware it was a good practice to consider one's behavior in advance, he thought it best to conduct first meetings between long-sundered branches of families with as much genuine spontaneity as possible. Mr. Collins's words bespoke an attempt to induce them to see him in as positive a light as possible which, while not precisely contemptible, could be interpreted as an attempt to hide the true man.

Such was not possible in Mr. Collins's case, thought Bennet as the family guided him into the house, the parson speaking incessantly of anything that crossed his mind. Nothing was beneath his notice, from the state of the servants' dress to the trinkets displayed on various surfaces to the slightest speck of dust. Indeed, given some of his . . . interesting pronouncements, Bennet thought anyone admitted to the chore of hearing him speak must understand his foolishness at once.

"What an excellent home you have, Cousin!" exclaimed Mr. Collins; the parson had retreated to his room to refresh himself but had emerged long before the family might have wished. "I might never have expected to see such harmony, such a perfect blend of economy and refinement gathered together in one house."

Mr. Collins looked around the sitting-room in which he sat, contemplating majesty and greatness only his eyes could see. "Might I ask which of your daughters is responsible for this heavenly room, and the cost of the renovations? It will be excellent information for when I must see to such concerns myself."

Before Bennet could comment, or even consider the many problems with the man's gauche question, Mr. Collins paled.

"Of course, I would not have you believe I do not already receive excellent instruction from my wondrous patroness, Lady Catherine de Bourgh. Her ladyship is all that is condescending and affable, such that I can scarce comprehend how my situation could be more fortunate. Her ladyship's guidance is without peer! Fine though your house is, it cannot compare with the grandeur of Rosings Park, of course."

"I understand your patroness is a widow," said Bennet, grasping at any means to alter the conversation.

"She is," confirmed Mr. Collins, a response so brief as to be almost sensible. His next words undid any progress he might have made. "Lady Catherine is, as you must understand, the most preeminent woman in Kent, and perhaps all of England!"

"More prominent than even Queen Charlotte?" murmured Bennet to himself. "Impressive."

Mr. Collins did not hear him. "She possesses taste so fine as to surpass all but deity, an instinctive knowledge of what is to be done in any situation, and attention to detail necessary to ensure all within reach of her influence are harmonious and content. Why, I do not know what I might do if she did not gift us with her boundless wisdom."

"Does she have any children?" asked Elizabeth.

The way Mr. Collins scowled at Elizabeth suggested he thought the question improper. "She had one daughter, but unfortunately, she was of an indifferent constitution and has returned to the courts on high. Though this must be a cruel blow to her ladyship, she endures it with patience and long-suffering."

Privately Bennet thought that "patience" and "long-suffering" were adjectives unlikely to describe the man's patroness. Given his character and the way he praised her to the skies, Bennet suspected the woman was meddling and dictatorial, a supposition supported by Darcy's words on the subject. Elizabeth, Bennet noted, watched the parson as if he were diseased, affronted by his anger at her innocent question. Bennet eyed her for a moment, but he did not concern himself, for he knew she would learn to laugh at the man's excesses and ignore his offenses.

The parson continued to blather on, his comments liberally sprinkled with such phrases as "Lady Catherine said . . ." or "It is Lady Catherine's opinion . . ." Such talk was of no interest to the assorted Bennets, but at least it diverted Collins from improper questions of the cost of the décor in the room or the quality of the fabric of his daughters' dresses. When faced with such absurdities as William Collins, Bennet supposed one had no choice but to accept such pyrrhic victories when they arose.

Dinner was not appreciably better. Mr. Collins was positively indefatigable, a fount of words fed by a spring that appeared bottomless. He spoke with equal fervor about silverware, the view from the window, and the superiority of the meal, even smacking his lips in appreciation frequently. Had he not watched the man eat more than any two of his daughters, he might not have thought Collins had time to pause from his continual vomit of words to push a morsel past his lips. He even asked after which of his daughters had prepared the meal, a question Bennet knew would have offended his departed wife.

"Longbourn employs a cook, Mr. Collins," said Elizabeth, her tone one of amusement rather than asperity, proving she had already seen the wisdom of taking nothing he said to heart. "My sisters and I are fortunate that we need not concern ourselves with such matters as cooking."

"Ah, that is well then," said the parson. "And fortunate for you, I am certain."

Then he launched into some useless account of Lady Catherine's instructions on the importance of servants, how much beef one must purchase, and some unfathomable discourse concerning the efficacy of beans in staving off gout. It was all incomprehensible to Bennet.

Jane, he noted, said little to the parson. All his daughters had been mostly silent, with Lizzy saying more than her sisters combined. Jane *was* reticent, he knew, but she could speak her mind when she felt it was worth her while. It appeared she had seen something in the parson's behavior that gave her pause and caused her to pull back and allow Elizabeth to speak for them all. Then Mr. Collins spoke, and Bennet realized what it was, and he wondered that he had not seen it before.

"It appears you have seen to the education of your excellent daughters, including the management of a house. That is wonderful, sir, for a widower in your position might have neglected such education. And as I have need . . ."

The parson paused and thought better of whatever he meant to say. "But of this, it would be best to demur, though I will return to the subject anon."

Then he turned his attention to something else. Bennet heard nothing of what he said, for he now knew what brought Mr. Collins to Longbourn. The man was searching for a wife.

Thus, Bennet's conundrum was clear. He was not in the habit of involving himself in others' affairs, preferring to sit back and watch, taking amusement where he could. Lizzy would accuse him of being a misanthrope, but Bennet had never known this approach to betray him.

Yet it was impossible to do nothing in this situation. He was his daughters' guardian, the man they relied upon to protect them, see to their happiness, and care for their needs. Bennet knew they were proof against anything his cousin could do. The man's means of wooing would no doubt be as inept as his attempts at conversation.

Thus, Bennet steeled himself to speak with Collins about his intentions. It may bring about the end of their new association, but Bennet could not consider that a loss. The man would become insufferable long before he would quit the house.

Had Elizabeth any notion that her father had not understood the parson's purpose in coming to Longbourn, she might not have been so angry. The man was unendurable as a guest, a fact that should have been clear to even one so dense as he. Kitty, never one for solitude and reflection, returned to her room as soon as she could that morning, and Mary took herself from the sitting-room to the back parlor where she could play on the small pianoforte in solitude. As her father had sequestered himself in his room, dealing with a matter of the estate, it fell to Elizabeth and Jane to entertain Mr. Collins, as leaving him alone would not have reflected well on them.

Much as he had the previous evening, Mr. Collins rambled on about anything that crossed his mind, his conversation so ubiquitous as to require no response. Elizabeth chose the simple expedient of ignoring him, as she could not imagine anything he might have to say that would interest her in the slightest. Then she noticed a pattern in his speech that informed her of the lay of the land, even if she had not understood his truncated comment when he made it.

"What say you, Cousin Jane?" said the parson, leaning toward her in a manner Elizabeth thought improper.

Having missed the subject of Mr. Collins's question, Elizabeth waited for Jane to respond. However, her sister only murmured: "I am certain you must be correct, Mr. Collins."

"Oh, most assuredly I am, for Lady Catherine has instructed me herself, and her ladyship cannot be mistaken. She is the wisest lady in all the land; I simply cannot wait until you meet her, for I know you shall think as I do."

This time Jane mumbled something that sounded noncommittal, not that the parson saw it for what it was.

"And Rosings Park itself! You shall see that it is a beautiful estate, not lacking in windows or topiaries, elegance in all its lines. It is a wondrous place; one I expect perfectly suited to your tastes.

"The parsonage is not so grand, of course," continued Mr. Collins. "But it is of excellent quality and was built only a decade ago by the order of Lady Catherine's dearly departed husband. It is eminently suitable for a man of my position, being neither too large nor too small. I also have servants, a woman to manage the house and another to clean, and a lady who comes to the parsonage to cook my meals."

"That is fortunate for you, Mr. Collins," replied Jane.

"It is!" crowed the parson. "I must attribute the excellence of my position to the guidance of my patroness, and any companion of mine must partake in her ladyship's gracious condescension. What a fortunate situation it will be! What happiness will be ours until we must take our rightful place as the owners of this excellent estate!"

At that moment, Jane turned an expression of pleading to Elizabeth. Jane, Elizabeth knew, was not incapable of defending herself. The situation demanded a response that would approach rudeness, and Jane did not have it within herself to be rude to *anyone*, even a man so silly and objectionable as William Collins.

While Elizabeth opened her mouth to rein in the excesses of Mr. Collins's speech and presumption, the door opened, and her father stepped into the room. He appeared to be in a remarkably good mood as he greeted them, asking after their morning, and informing them he had completed his business. Then he turned to Mr. Collins.

"I hope my daughters have provided for your entertainment, sir."

"Oh, without a doubt!" exclaimed Mr. Collins. "I have been regaling Miss Bennet with tales of my home and the sights of Rosings Park, the home of my dear patroness. I do not think I have disappointed her with what I have said."

It was on Elizabeth's mind to be cross with her father. She had seen how he had comprehended Mr. Collins's purpose the previous evening, and yet he had done nothing to restrain the man's ardor. It would be just like him to sit back and enjoy the fun, taking no thought for his daughters' discomfort. Elizabeth was not about to sit still for this behavior.

Elizabeth saw in a moment she had misjudged him, for when the parson spoke, Mr. Bennet's countenance fell. Through the continual jabbering, he directed serious looks, first at the parson, then at Jane and Elizabeth in turn. After looking at Jane, his gaze softened, and he turned a wry look on Elizabeth, complete with a heavenward glance. Then he turned his attention back on the parson, his expression growing severe, sending the balm of relief to Elizabeth's cooling annoyance.

"It is well that you have so comfortable a situation, Mr. Collins," said Mr. Bennet, springing into an imperceptible pause in his cousin's words to forestall them. "Now, perhaps you would like to join me in my study, so we may speak of a few matters of import."

The way the parson glanced at Jane showed his reluctance to depart, but then he turned a knowing look on her father and accepted with alacrity. No doubt the dullard thought her father meant to offer his daughter to him on a silver platter. Elizabeth once again witnessed her father's exasperation as he rose and drew the parson along with him as he departed the room. For a moment, Elizabeth and Jane remained in silence, the distant sounds of Mary on the pianoforte accompanying their thoughts.

Then the door opened, and Kitty stepped into the room. "I saw Papa lead Mr. Collins to his study," fretted the girl. "I hope he does not mean to require one of us to marry him."

"No, Kitty," said Jane, beckoning Kitty to her at once. Kitty went to her, burrowing into Jane's side as she had done as a young girl. "I dare say it is quite the opposite."

"Oh, that is a relief!" cried she. "I could not imagine enduring such a man for the rest of my life! It is altogether unfathomable."

"I cannot agree more, Kitty," said Elizabeth kindly. "Jane is correct about Papa's intention. But let us not forget to keep ourselves under good regulation. Mr. Collins is difficult to endure, but it would not do to offend him."

Kitty nodded, and they dropped the subject. Hopefully, when Mr. Collins departed their father's library, he would not consider one of them his for the taking. If he did not heed her father's counsel, Elizabeth was prepared to take a hand herself, whether she would offend him or not.

"What excellent daughters you have, Cousin!" exclaimed Mr. Collins when they reached the sanctuary of his room. "What loveliness and breeding, what modesty and delicacy. Why, though tales of their quality traveled before them, I never would have imagined the reality.

"Miss Bennet is the loveliest creature I have ever beheld. I am the most fortunate man alive!"

Bennet watched his cousin, his annoyance growing with every ridiculous statement, with every unwanted exclamation. For a time, while the man continued to extol the virtues of Bennet's daughters and his own good fortune, Bennet considered the relative benefits of simply depositing him in the dust of the driveway and instructing him to leave and never return. It was tempting—oh, so tempting.

Appealing though it was, Bennet knew it would not be wise. This caricature of a man was, for good or ill, his heir, the man who would be the next steward of his family's legacy. Given his general lack of sense or ability, Bennet had little hope the estate would survive his cousin's stupidity. But to send him on his way without trying to impart a little sense was unconscionable. Thus, it was incumbent on Bennet to treat with his cousin; the first thing he must know was that he would not have the choice of whichever Bennet daughter he desired.

"Yes, Mr. Collins," said Bennet, reflecting that inserting oneself into his never-ending waterfall of words was an acquired skill, "I understand you appreciate my daughters. Thank you for your praise, for they are good girls if I say so myself. I am prodigiously proud of them."

"So, you must be!" cried the parson. "For they are paragons—"

"Precisely the word I would have used," interrupted Bennet, losing patience. "It seems you have come to Longbourn with a purpose beyond that of simply healing the breach or viewing your future inheritance. Will you not tell me what you wish from us?"

"To speak of such things precipitously is not proper," said Mr. Collins, trying to demur.

"On the contrary," replied Bennet before the man could continue speaking, ignoring how Collins had already broken his own scruples, "I believe it is best to understand each other without the possibility for error. It will help avoid misapprehension later."

The parson regarded him for a long moment, perhaps the longest he had ever gone without speaking in Bennet's presence. Then he nodded, perhaps indicating a decision.

"You are correct, of course. It is most sensible of you, Cousin, for I would also not wish misunderstanding to arise between us."

Bennet nodded, but he judged it would be best if the parson broached the subject first. "To that end, perhaps you should state your reasons for coming to Longbourn."

"Of course," agreed Mr. Collins. "My reasons are exactly what I informed you in my letter, Cousin, for it is not only appropriate that I should see my future home but as Lady Catherine has so graciously observed: 'disharmony between families cannot endure, for there is nothing worse than those, who should be united in purpose, opposed in contention.' I am, as you must already apprehend, resolved to pursue her ladyship's guidance to action.

"But this was not the only advice Lady Catherine condescended to give me. 'Mr. Collins,' said she, 'it is not appropriate that you remain a bachelor, for it is the duty of all men of the cloth to set the example of matrimony to the parish over which they preside.' As always, her ladyship's encouragement is without peer, and when I spoke of you and your family, she further recommended I seek a wife among your daughters, so that I may succor them on that unhappy day when you join your companion in life in the eternal courts on high and I inherit all this estate."

His cousin was truly admirable, thought Bennet, as he valiantly sought to control his mirth. Whatever else happened, Bennet hoped he would keep his cousin's acquaintance, for his correspondence would provide Bennet with no end of amusement. Of the man's company, Bennet required little before he would become fatigued. But letters? Bennet would even essay to respond in a timely fashion if only to ensure a continual flow of his absurd observations.

"You wish to marry one of my daughters," said Bennet, seeking to clarify while he mastered himself.

"Miss Bennet, to be precise," said Mr. Collins. "I cannot imagine a better companion or a lovelier woman than she."

"Ah, then it is well we have had this conversation, Cousin, for I am afraid that is not possible." The parson gaped in astonishment, allowing Bennet to use his stupefaction to elaborate. "You see, there is a man recently arrived in the neighborhood who has paid her the compliment of his attention. While I cannot say without hesitation that it will lead to a match, I am certain Jane favors him. I cannot ask her to give up the object of her affection in favor of your suit."

Mr. Collins's brows drew down into a frown. "Yes, I can see that. I would not wish to interfere with such critical matters of the heart." Then Mr. Collins's expression brightened. "Then Miss Elizabeth will do. She is not so comely as her sister, but in behavior, she is everything genteel. She will serve as an adequate substitute."

It bore no worthy mention that to speak of a woman in such terms was hardly a way to make her fall violently in love.

"Unfortunately," said Bennet, by now enjoying himself, "Elizabeth is similarly engaged in a dance of courtship of her own. The man of whom I spoke, the man paying attention to Jane, has a friend who appears similarly infatuated with Elizabeth. The same impediment exists in her case."

Dumbfounded, the parson tried: "Mary —"

"Is too young," interrupted Bennet.

"Yes, I know she is nineteen, Cousin," said Bennet before his cousin could speak again, "but she is yet unready for marriage. I hope you will trust my judgment in this matter. By that same token, Kitty is also too young to marry."

Now, Mr. Collins was angry. "But Cousin. I came to Longbourn in good faith, ready to admire your daughters and choose from among them the companion of my future life. I might ask why you summarily reject my olive branch in a manner so little reflecting civility."

"It is not a lack of civility, Cousin," said Bennet. "Nor do I reject your olive branch, for I have gratefully accepted it. I only speak of the reality of the situation."

"But what will become of your excellent daughters when you leave this mortal life?" demanded Collins. "Without a closer connection to them, do you suppose I will support them in your absence? What will come of my solemn promise to Lady Catherine to return having achieved a sanctioned engagement?"

"While we can, none of us, know the time of our passing," replied Bennet, not bothering to hide his enjoyment and ignoring Collins's concern for his patroness's displeasure, "I do not believe I have one foot in the grave just yet. Besides, I spoke of two gentlemen admiring my eldest daughters; it would not surprise me if their appreciation led to marriage.

"Even should the worst happen, they are not so vulnerable as you suppose. I have provided for their future; they shall not be wealthy, but they will have the necessary means to support themselves."

Mr. Collins was floundering. It was a situation in which the parson found himself often, Bennet thought, but now it rendered him mute. While such a situation was desirable, Bennet knew he could not allow it to persist, for he truly did not wish to offend the man.

"Cousin, I mean no insult. You stated you have come to admire my daughters, and I appreciate the sentiment and your intention of putting yourself in a position where you may provide for them.

"At the same time, I was not false in my assertion of the reality of the situation. Jane and Elizabeth are not available, and Mary and Kitty are not ready to be married at present. Many other suitable young ladies would make fine wives. Shall you not turn your attention to someone else? Given your thoughtful consideration for my girls, I shall not take offense if you do."

Collins was not certain if he should take offense himself—that much was clear. While he regarded Bennet for several long moments, unspeaking, trying to comprehend, in the end, he came to the correct conclusion.

"I suppose you are correct, Cousin." He paused and then asked: "Are there any young ladies in this district who might suit?"

Relief flooded through Bennet. "There are. We shall be certain to introduce you."

After a few moments, Collins went away, leaving Bennet to the satisfaction of knowing he had done what he must to both protect his daughters and placate his guest. He hoped that nothing else would arise to complicate his life. Dealing with his cousin's foolishness was quite enough for the present.

CHAPTER VII

*F*rustration was a concept with which Louisa Hurst was well familiar. Much of it came with having a sister who was determined to go her own way and listen to nothing she, or anyone else, said. Part of it was watching said sister when she exasperated herself against her problems. This time in Hertfordshire was trending toward disaster, and it was not for the reason the Caroline suggested.

"What can we do?" muttered her sister as she paced the room in front of Louisa, who occupied a chair and wished she could depart. "Charles has always been so pliable, and yet he seems determined to throw his lot in with the little chit. And Mr. Darcy! He truly seems to appreciate that hoyden, Miss Elizabeth. I would never have expected such a lack of discernment from him!"

Caroline had not directed her comments at Louisa, and Louisa felt no motivation to reply. It was often thus, for Caroline had a habit of speaking her thoughts out loud when she thought no one of any importance would overhear. Louisa had long been accustomed to the notion that her sister did not truly care for her opinion, that she considered Louisa a tool to use to get what she wished. Her regard for her sister had become so damaged that Louisa did not concern herself with Caroline's opinion.

"Louisa, dear," said Caroline at length in that condescending tone Louisa found so tiresome, "it is on my mind that I should like to have some company tonight."

"The gentlemen are to attend a dinner with the officers."

"Yes. Therefore, it is safe to invite Miss Bennet, as we will not be putting her in Charles's way by doing so."

Louisa regarded her sister, suspicion for Caroline's motives overflowing. "Why do you propose to have Miss Bennet to dinner? As I recall, you have had little to say about her or her family that was not condemnation."

"No reason in particular," said Caroline, her studied nonchalance no screen for her scheming. "Jane *is* among the more tolerable in this miserable community, and she is certainly better than anyone else in her family. Remaining alone tonight in each other's company is not palatable and may lead to an argument. I should rather have someone with whom to converse, for I should like to know more about her."

With that, Caroline revealed her objective in inviting Miss Bennet, though Louisa had already guessed it. No one deserved to be probed for information that might condemn them in Caroline's eyes, least of all a sweet girl like Miss Jane Bennet. But Louisa was not of a mind to oppose her sister's design for the simple reason that she could not imagine suffering Caroline's company alone. Perhaps she would learn more of Miss Bennet herself, a desirable outcome as Louisa was becoming convinced that Miss Bennet would be her future sister.

"I have no objection," said Louisa. "I should be happy to welcome Miss Bennet tonight."

Caroline shot a look at her which suggested suspicion. In the end, however, she said nothing and dispatched a note with a footman a few moments later.

"It is from Miss Bingley. She has invited me to dinner this evening at Netherfield."

Regarding her sister, Elizabeth wondered at Miss Bingley's game. That she had no care for anyone of the Bennet family, least of all the neighborhood, she made abundantly clear to them all. What Miss Bingley might now mean by making overtures of friendship to Jane was something Elizabeth could not quite grasp.

"Do you mean to accept it?" asked Mr. Bennet.

Situated on the far side of the table during their luncheon, Mr. Bennet watched his eldest daughter, a hint of concern displayed on his otherwise passive countenance. Her father was as aware as any of them of Miss Bingley's disdain for his family.

"It would be rude to demur," replied Jane slowly.

"I do not understand," said Mr. Collins. "Why would you not accept such an invitation sent in friendship and good faith?"

"Because, Cousin," said Mr. Bennet, "there is some question as to the lady's sincerity."

It was clear Mr. Collins did not understand.

"The lady is new to the neighborhood," explained Mr. Bennet, seemingly trying to be as brief as possible. "She displays certain . . . tendencies toward excessive pride and disdain for those who call this community our home. What she means in this instance, I cannot say, but our history with her does not promote trust."

Mr. Collins nodded, allowing Mr. Bennet to turn his attention to Jane. "What say you, Jane? If I am not mistaken, I believe Miss Bingley has been kinder toward you than anyone else in the neighborhood."

"I do not trust her, Papa," replied Jane, a shocking reply that Elizabeth would not have predicted, even given her sure knowledge of Jane's understanding gained the night of the dinner at Longbourn. "But I recognize her as Mr. Bingley's sister, a woman with whom I may need to foster good relations."

"At the same time, Jane," said Elizabeth, "she would not have invited you now, on a night when the gentleman will not be at home, if she did not have some purpose in mind."

"Ah, yes, the dinner with the officers." Mr. Bennet looked to Mr. Collins. "That had slipped my mind, Cousin. You will, of course, attend with me."

Left unsaid was how Mr. Collins could not stay at Longbourn with only the younger Bennet sisters in attendance. Whether the parson understood that point, she could not say, but he nodded readily enough.

"Even so," continued Jane, "I would not insult Miss Bingley by refusing to attend her." Jane paused and smiled. "It is not as if we Bennets have secrets we must hide. I am certain I will escape unscathed."

"I cannot imagine you are not equal to anything she might attempt," said Bennet, regarding his eldest with ready affection. "Then we may call it settled. The only question is the arrangements to convey you to Netherfield, considering our need to go to Meryton."

Later that day, Jane boarded Longbourn's coach for the journey to Netherfield, with Mr. Bennet and Mr. Collins. The gentleman would debark at the militia's headquarters in Meryton, and the coach would then proceed on to Netherfield. Then they would return in reverse order. Elizabeth did not expect her sister to experience much pleasure that evening with the sisters, but she knew Jane had made the correct decision to go.

As the carriage retreated into the oncoming gloom of dusk, Elizabeth turned to her two younger sisters. "It appears we are alone this evening."

"And free of Mr. Collins!" said Kitty, showing her sisters a wide grin.

"That benefit cannot be underestimated," added Mary, the sister most likely to tolerate Mr. Collins's eccentricities.

"Indeed," replied Elizabeth. "I do not know how I shall bear the deprivation."

Laughing together, the sisters entered the house to partake of their meal. Elizabeth was closer to Jane than she was to anyone else in the world, but she also enjoyed her other sisters' company. It was a quiet evening, in which they strengthened the bonds between them.

By the time Jane and their father returned, the three remaining sisters had already retired for the evening. This was as much because of the desire to avoid Mr. Collins as for any fatigue. Jane did not knock on Elizabeth's door, and Elizabeth was content with learning what happened at Netherfield the following morning.

When she arose, Elizabeth greeted her family cheerfully at breakfast after a short constitutional about the estate. It was clear at once that Jane was more than a little pensive. That was not unusual, for Jane was often quiet and introspective. On that morning, however, Elizabeth could only attribute it to her previous evening in the company of a viper.

"Jane?" asked Mr. Bennet, seeing what Elizabeth had in Jane's demeanor. "Was your dinner with the Bingley ladies last night enjoyable?"

Mustering a wan smile, Jane nodded. "It was a pleasant evening. The meal was excellent, and the ladies were very attentive."

"Yet, I can see that something bothers you."

Jane sighed and nodded. "There is. Mrs. Hurst was everything friendly and obliging; I enjoyed her company. As for Miss Bingley . . ." The ensuing pause was awful to the feelings of them all. "At first Miss Bingley was kind and gracious, but after a time, she began to ask probing questions."

"Questions?" prompted Mr. Bennet. Elizabeth could see that he already suspected what Jane would tell him.

"About our position in society, our connections, the extent of our dowries, and other such intrusive queries."

"That is not unexpected," murmured Mr. Bennet. "I would not expect a woman such as she to avoid such gauche queries about the extent of one's fortune."

Mr. Collins's eyes shot to Mr. Bennet, apparently surprised at his statement. But Mr. Bennet ignored him.

"Then I suppose you informed them of the Gardiners and the Phillipses?"

Jane's gaze found her father. "I am not ashamed of our relations, Papa. I would not treat them as embarrassing secrets."

"No, Jane, nor would I expect it of you." Mr. Bennet sighed and shook his head. "But that was precisely the reason for Miss Bingley's invitation, or I am no judge at all."

"Forgive me, Mr. Bennet," said Mr. Collins, "but I do not understand. Why do you suppose this Miss Bingley would shun you for your relations?"

"Because, by society's standards, they are not considered fashionable," replied Mr. Bennet, pushing back in his chair. "Mr. Gardiner is my departed wife's brother, and Mrs. Phillips, her sister. Mr. Gardiner is a man of trade, while Mr. Phillips is the town's solicitor. To a woman as proud as Miss Bingley, they would be insupportable connections, for she yearns to rise to the heights of society."

"If you will pardon my saying," said Mr. Collins, "that stinks of pride and covetousness."

"I cannot say you are incorrect." Mr. Bennet paused, regarding his cousin. "I would not teach you to despise Miss Bingley, Cousin; you have not met our neighbors yet. You will be in their company ere you depart. Yet I can also not pretend Miss Bingley's behavior is above reproach. I ask you to reserve comment within her company, for it is not good manners to abuse another in their presence, even if their behavior warrants it."

His uncertainty remained, but Mr. Collins did nothing other than nod his assent.

"What do you suppose she means to do with this knowledge, Papa?" asked Jane.

"What do *you* suppose she will do, Jane?" demanded Elizabeth. "No doubt she is, even now, attempting to persuade the gentlemen away from us."

"Miss Bingley's brother is your admirer?" asked Mr. Collins, his face now permanently etched with shock.

"Surely they will not listen," said Jane, her concern now overflowing. With her reply, Mr. Collins had his answer.

"In that, I think you have little reason to concern yourself." Mr. Bennet gave his eldest an encouraging smile. "Darcy is not one to give Miss Bingley any consequence; I suspect he does not care much for her. As for Bingley, it appears he is long accustomed to ignoring his sister. All Miss Bingley's efforts will avail her nothing."

While it was clear she was uncertain, Jane nodded, still distressed. Mr. Bennet would not allow her to fret.

"There is little reason to reproach yourself, Jane. If Miss Bingley had asked anyone in town, she would have received this information about us. As you said, we are not ashamed of our relations, nor will we attempt to deny them. Let Miss Bingley act as she will; if she persuades the gentlemen against you, they are not deserving of you, anyway. It is of little matter."

With that, they dropped the subject and returned to their meal. In time, when they had finished, they left the table, each to their pursuits. Mr. Bennet, Elizabeth noted, invited Mr. Collins to join him in his study, then suggested a ride about the estate, so he may learn something of his future home. Mr. Collins readily assented, though he remained in the dining room after his host quit it. The looks he directed at Jane and Elizabeth were curious, and Elizabeth could not imagine what he meant by them. Then he spoke and removed all question.

"Cousin Jane, Cousin Elizabeth," said he, his manner formal even for him. "Your father has spoken of your admirers and warned me against involving myself. I have never met these men who hold your esteem and cannot say what will come of this Miss Bingley's interference. Should your gentlemen fail you, I shall put myself forward for your consideration, though I am but a poor substitute."

"Thank you, Mr. Collins," said Jane, speaking before Elizabeth could muster a response. "We appreciate your assurances."

With a bow and a hint of a smile, the parson departed, the sound of the door to their father's study closing echoing in his wake. When she believed he could not overhear her, Elizabeth turned an arched brow on Jane.

"Perhaps you shall have an admirer, even if Mr. Bingley proves false."

"Do you suppose he will?"

Elizabeth considered the question. "Mr. Bingley has struck me as possessing a complying temper, but I do not believe he allows his sister to rule him. *If* the gentlemen admire us, I suspect my situation is more secure than yours, for I have ample proof that Mr. Darcy does not like Miss Bingley and will not listen to her. For what it is worth, I suspect Mr. Bingley will not allow her to sway him either."

"That is my interpretation too." Jane smiled and gave her a wan smile. "If he proves false, I think you know I will remain unmoved by Mr. Collins's assurances. Regardless, I believe his words were kindly meant."

Elizabeth agreed with her sister. Perhaps there was more to Mr. Collins than the ridiculousness she had attributed to him. That did not mean she wished to have him as a husband.

Self-satisfaction, thy name is Caroline Bingley. Had he known of the discussion at Longbourn, he might have tipped his cap to their perception of his friend's sister. Yet, he did not, and the knowledge of her reason for her sense of superiority would not come until later that day.

The ladies had already retired by the time the men had returned to the estate, an unlooked-for boon, yet one for which Darcy had been grateful. Since Miss Bingley had joined them that morning, she had shown a sense of haughty complacency, such that Darcy now thought she had purposely avoided them the previous evening, though he could not determine the reason for it. There was little doubt it had to do with Miss Bennet's visit the previous evening, but beyond that fact, he could not guess what she was about.

As he did not much care for her brand of arrogance, Darcy avoided her that morning, knowing she would choose the most advantageous time to relay the contents of her thoughts. Until she chose to do so, Darcy had little notion of enduring her company. The woman finally made her sentiments known when they came together for dinner, though it was not without strife.

"Caroline, Louisa," said Bingley, addressing his sisters with a manner absent. "I have been considering how best to thank our new friends for the ready welcome we have enjoyed since we came to Netherfield. After some thought, I have determined that I should like to host a ball."

"A ball?" demanded Miss Bingley at once. "Why do you wish to hold a ball? Do you suppose *anything* will impart a bit of culture to these people? You may as well try your hand at teaching a pig to dance."

"Yet, I am resolved," said Bingley, apparently unconcerned by his sister's vitriol. "It is the perfect way to express our appreciation."

Bingley turned and regarded his sister. "Please consider this: the estates in this neighborhood are too small for balls, and Netherfield has been empty for some years. There likely has not been a private ball since the last time this estate was occupied. As you have never planned such an event, this will allow you to spread your wings in a location where those who attend will feel naught but gratitude for our largesse, rather than the judging stares of those in town."

The best way to get his way was to appeal to Miss Bingley's vanity; Darcy thought his friend had given her an irresistible lure. Miss Bingley would complain about it for some time, but she would capitulate. Her minute glance in his direction further proved his opinion. But Darcy was lacking some piece of the puzzle, for Miss Bingley did not act the way he had supposed.

"I do not think hosting a ball is at all wise," said she with a sniff of utter disdain. "In fact, I cannot but think it would be best to return to town at once."

"I have already said I will not go to town," said Bingley. "I am fixed at Netherfield, Caroline. There is nothing you can say that will change my mind."

"I am convinced you will understand when I tell you what I have learned."

The siblings stared at each other in a contest of wills. It was not apparent who emerged the victor, for after a moment, Bingley said: "What do you mean?"

"Only that the supposed leading family of the neighborhood has proven just as base as the rest."

"I assume you refer to the Bennets," said Bingley wearily, guessing the thrust of Miss Bingley's claim as quickly as Darcy did himself. "I tire of your conceit, Caroline. There is nothing wrong with the Bennets."

"You would not say as much if you knew," said Caroline, her manner faintly triumphant.

Bingley showed his fatigue in the massaging of his temples. "I am certain you have gaged the most devastating time to inform us, Caroline. I might have known you had some ulterior motive in inviting Miss Bennet to dine with you." Bingley turned to his elder sister. "I suppose you were involved in Caroline's schemes?"

"I know no harm of the Bennets, Brother. Caroline's actions were her own."

With a nod and a half-smile to Mrs. Hurst, Bingley turned back to his younger sister, who was seething by this time. "So, what is it, Caroline? Do the Bennets have some dark secret that exposes them all? Perhaps they are French spies planted in England by the tyrant's foresight to wreak havoc on us all? Or do they have a parson or other equally unsuitable relation?"

"If you recall," said Darcy, "they *do* have a relation who is a parson."

"Yes," said Bingley wryly. "I remember, Darcy."

"A parson *is* an unfortunate connection, indeed," said an enraged Miss Bingley. The way she clenched and unclenched her talons, Darcy wondered if she wished to fly at her brother, rake at him with claws extended. "But that is not the worst of it. Mrs. Bennet was not a gentlewoman, for her father was naught but the town's solicitor, a position now held by their aunt's husband."

"A respectable profession," observed Darcy.

Miss Bingley glared at him, but she did not allow her momentum to wane. "But that is not even the worst. Their uncle is a man of *business* who owns a *shop* in London. They have close connections to *trade*, connections Miss Bennet did not even attempt to deny."

"Oh, Caroline," said Hurst, shaking his head and chuckling to himself. "How you can remain blind to your hypocritical lack of self-awareness is beyond my understanding."

"How you can continue as a drunken sod is beyond mine," rasped Caroline. Her glare encompassed them all. "I cannot understand you. If we are to gain acceptance in society, we cannot connect ourselves to such people."

"Do you forget the source of *our* wealth?" asked Bingley with no little disgust.

"I do not!" exclaimed she, though her longing to forget it was plain in every syllable spilling from her mouth. "We have *left* trade behind. Our father charged us with improving the family's position in society. We cannot do so if we accept unsuitable connections."

"I shall not allow you to draw me into a debate about what our father wished of us," said Bingley. "Suffice it to say that your conclusions are nonsensical. Father understood that the purchase of an estate would not grant us admittance to the highest echelons of society. We will always be new money to many of that set."

"But even such status as we have will evaporate with a connection to a *tradesman!*" Miss Bingley spat the word like an epithet. "Tell him,

Mr. Darcy! Remind him that our advancement requires gaining the right connections."

"I apologize, Miss Bingley," replied Darcy. "But I do not have such influence over your brother, for he may do as he chooses. I have no notion Bingley's feelings toward Miss Bennet have developed to that extent, but if they have, I will do nothing more than wish him joy."

Miss Bingley stared at him, unable to comprehend what he said. It was, he suspected, the first time she had ever acknowledged the fact that she might not possess the influence to bend her brother to her will. Perhaps she might now consider the possibility Darcy himself would not fall in with her designs. Inevitably, she would discover it, though Darcy was not yet prepared for the consequences of her understanding.

"Leave off, Caroline," said Bingley. "I shall not depart from Netherfield until I am ready, and I shall make my own choices when it pertains to my life and happiness. If you do not appreciate my choices, I suggest you absent yourself from my company."

To leave Netherfield was not palatable. Her eyes did not find Darcy, but he knew he was most prominent in her mind. For how would she continue her attempts to entrap him if she were not in his presence?

"Of course, Brother," said she, her voice as sweet and sickening as saccharine. "It is merely my concern for you that has led me to speak. If you wish to hold a ball, I shall, of course, plan it for you."

She did not make any further attempt to degrade the people her brother proposed to host. Darcy was instantly suspicious. No doubt she wished to use the ball to achieve her end of separating her brother from Miss Bennet. Or at least to prove to Darcy how competent she was and what an excellent wife she would make him.

Regardless, Darcy resolved to take even greater care. There might be many opportunities for her to attempt to force his hand during an evening of dancing. Should she succeed, Darcy was determined to refuse any entreaty to honor his supposed obligations as a gentleman. To do so would bring about his ruin, to demean him by consigning him to life with a bitter shrew as a wife. That was something he would not do.

"What do you think of Caroline's capitulation?" asked Bingley later that evening when the ladies had retired.

"I think she has some other stratagem in mind," said Darcy.

Bingley chuckled. "Observant as always, my friend. I shall not advise you, as you have been avoiding snares since you entered society. Caroline *is* my sister, after all."

"For that, Bingley, you have my condolences."

Bingley guffawed, and they bid each other good night. The problem of Miss Bingley could wait until the morrow.

CHAPTER VIII

*M*eryton was not an exciting place. It was a small collection of weather-beaten buildings along a principal street which was still a dirt track rather than cobblestones, a street that became muddy and all but impassible when it rained. Even to the locals, there was little of interest in Meryton other than a few modest shops serving the surrounding gentlefolk, a small assembly hall set aside for their use, and the few relations one or another of the gentleman could boast among the townsfolk. Mr. Phillips, the town's solicitor, and Mrs. Phillips, sister to the former Mrs. Bennet, were prominent among such connections.

Of little interest though it was, Meryton was the nearest village of any size in the neighborhood, close enough that the younger generation of gentlefolk often met there. No matter how many times they perused the shops and lamented as to the paucity of their wares, they kept returning, for ennui was a curious affliction. Of course, of late, the company of militia quartered in the town added to its appeal, such that one could not walk ten paces without encountering a pocket of red-clad officers, flirting with young maidens of the neighborhood. The officers were also popular among the more credulous of the young men of the district, who often listened to those intrepid adventurers' stories, nary a thought of whether they were true passing through their minds.

The Bennet sisters were no less immune to the uncertain lure of Meryton than any other ladies in the neighborhood. They often walked thither, together or alone, visited with their aunt, or investigated the shops, breathlessly hoping their stock had somehow changed from the previous time they had entered. The Bennets were not as enamored with the officers as many others, as Jane was indifferent, Mary disapproving, and Elizabeth only interested insomuch as those fine fellows might provide new subjects for character study. The one Bennet sister, Kitty, who was inclined to give those gentlemen what they considered their due, was yet young, and her elder sisters, knowing her character, remained vigilant whenever she was in their company.

One could hardly remain unknown to the officers unless one completely eschewed the events of the neighborhood, for the homes of the local gentlemen teemed with red-coated men. A few among them Elizabeth found interesting, and she did not refrain from speaking to them when the opportunity arose. Such was the case a few mornings after Jane's evening with the Bingley sisters.

That morning all four Bennet sisters agreed to walk to the town, and in this desire, Mr. Collins joined them. The parson, while they might rightly have thought his visit would be unendurable, had settled into the house, his time largely dominated by Mr. Bennet's efforts to show him something of his future inheritance. Elizabeth sensed her father had grown fatigued with Mr. Collins's company, and the parson, as he now did not look on his cousin's daughters as potential brides, appeared to be suffering from a lack of anything with which to occupy himself.

"A walk to Meryton sounds like just the thing, Cousin Elizabeth," intoned he when he learned of the outing. "Should we come across an acquaintance of yours, I should be happy to request an introduction."

"Then to Meryton we shall go," said Elizabeth, ignoring his comment about her friends. She could not think of one of them that would tolerate Mr. Collins's silliness for more than a moment or two.

The walkers all donned their outerwear, accepted bonnets, hats, and gloves from the attending servants, and soon they made their way outside for the mile walk to Meryton. Whatever Mr. Collins said about his propensity to walk about the parsonage or his patroness's estate — Rosings Park being a subject of which he had spoken at great length — it was clear at once the man was no walker. Whether it was his rounded belly or his spindly legs, he was puffing and mopping his forehead within moments of their departure, such that she wondered if he would pass out from exhaustion before they even reached Lucas Lodge.

Mr. Collins showed himself equal to the task, however, staying with them until they reached the town some time later. There, the ubiquitous flamboyance of the officers' uniforms drew all eyes to them, and Kitty fidgeted as if she would have gone at once had her sisters not been present. In particular, Elizabeth caught sight of a single officer, one better known to them than the rest, who marched up the street alone. It could not be said that any of those fine fellows were of an unsociable disposition, and this man did not walk past them without stopping and offering a hearty greeting.

"Miss Bennet," said Mr. Denny, bowing low, his face wearing his habitual grin. "Miss Elizabeth, Miss Mary, Miss Kitty. How do you do this fine morning?"

"We do very well, Mr. Denny," replied Elizabeth, speaking for her sisters. "I understand you were in London recently?"

"Aye, I just returned this morning," replied he. "It is unfortunate, for I might have brought a new acquaintance with me. But my friend decided at the last moment not to accept a commission in the regiment."

"That is shocking!" exclaimed Elizabeth with a grin. "I hope you abused him for his wastrel ways, Mr. Denny."

The officer returned Elizabeth's grin. "I am certain his ears are ringing with the sound of my reprimand even now. To think that a man would not do his duty and protect such charming ladies as yourselves from the French!"

"Have you heard anything of an invasion?"

They all laughed together at Elizabeth's jest, though she thought Mr. Collins had not understood her irony.

"Nothing so terrible," replied Mr. Denny. "In fact, I believe our forces are gaining the upper hand.

"But if you will excuse me, I have an appointment I must keep. I hope I shall be in your company again very soon."

The ladies all agreed, and with a few more words he went away. At once, Kitty turned on Elizabeth.

"Lizzy!" whined she. "How will I come to know the officers if you dominate their conversation?"

"That is a matter about which I have little concern, Kitty," said Elizabeth, throwing her sister a quelling glare. "You have a tongue if you choose to use it, and we were in Mr. Denny's company for several minutes. As for knowing the officers better, I think you know them as well as you should, given your age."

Kitty huffed her annoyance, but in the face of Mary's disapproving frown and Jane's more pointed one, she desisted. Mr. Collins, Elizabeth noted, looked on them with approval, and Kitty with a measure of censure. But he said nothing, which Elizabeth appreciated, knowing he would only anger her youngest sister.

For a time, the sisters toured the shops, as was their wont, Mr. Collins departing for a short time to visit Meryton's church. His absence was no hardship to the sisters, who were more than capable of seeing to their amusement; such amusement as Meryton boasted was more readily obtained when he was not with them. It was not long before they were to return to Longbourn that Elizabeth caught sight of a dear friend.

"Charlotte!" exclaimed she, moving to greet her. "Had we known you were to walk to Meryton, we might have called at Lucas Lodge before we came."

"It is no trouble, Lizzy," replied Charlotte. "I am here on a commission for my mother."

Before Elizabeth responded, Mr. Collins interrupted: "Cousin Elizabeth, will you do me the honor of introducing me to your friend?"

Charlotte was the only acquaintance they had come across while in Mr. Collins's company, which must account for his eagerness. Assenting, Elizabeth performed the introductions, her raised eyebrow at her friend where the parson could not see conveying her opinion of their guest. Charlotte, though she noted it, greeted Mr. Collins with perfect civility, allowing the parson to engage her in conversation. Elizabeth might have joined in, but the arrival of the two gentlemen from Netherfield distracted her.

"Miss Bennet!" exclaimed Mr. Bingley as he vaulted from his saddle. "How fortunate we are to have come across you, for we were going to Longbourn to visit you and your family."

Elizabeth might have taken more interest in Jane's conversation with Mr. Bingley, but Mr. Darcy stood before her. In a teasing tone, she addressed the gentleman, saying: "Had you missed us, you could have visited with my father."

"That is true, Miss Elizabeth," said he. "But your father is not as interesting as his daughters."

Showing the man a raised eyebrow, she chuckled when he winked at her. Thereafter, she stood for several moments speaking with him, though their position in the middle of Meryton's busiest street was by no means conducive to a meaningful discussion. As they talked, Elizabeth noted two rather interesting things, both of which included Mr. Collins. The first was that Charlotte was speaking with the man and keeping him with her, though Mr. Collins was watching Mr. Darcy and Mr. Bingley. The second was that Mr. Collins regarded the gentlemen with an almost critical air.

Now, why would he look at them with disfavor?

Darcy had noticed Mr. Collins's behavior the night of the dinner with the officers. Knowing what sort of man he was—and confirming his suspicions within moments of being in his company—Darcy might have thought Collins would lavish the same fawning attention on him that he did on Lady Catherine. Yet Mr. Collins remained aloof, watching them through cool eyes, his manner almost disapproving. It appeared Bennet had not informed him of Darcy's identity, for which Darcy was grateful. He might have been happy to keep matters that way, but perhaps it was too much to ask.

The first moments of the parson's sudden comprehension escaped Darcy's attention, for he had focused on Miss Elizabeth Bennet to the exclusion of all others. Whether Collins had recalled his name—he had no doubt Lady Catherine had spoken of him—Darcy could not say. The man's utter stupefaction confronted him, forcing Darcy to take notice.

"Mr. Darcy?" demanded he, awe dripping from his tone. "Mr. *Fitzwilliam* Darcy of Pemberley in Derbyshire?"

Knowing at once what must ensue and cursing his ill luck, Darcy turned to Collins and nodded. "Yes, I am he. We were introduced the other night, were we not?"

A sudden paleness, that of a snowdrift in winter, fell over Collins's mien. "I apologize . . . ! Why, I was not . . . I had no notion . . . Why did you not tell me you were Lady Catherine de Bourgh's nephew?"

"I apologize, Mr. Collins," said Darcy, now diverted, noting how Miss Elizabeth had raised her hand to her mouth to hide a laugh. "I was not aware that I must account for all my relations when making an acquaintance."

That drew Mr. Collins up short. Unfortunately, that state of affairs persisted for only a few moments.

"No, of course, you could not have known. Mr. Darcy, I am the incumbent of the position of parson to her ladyship."

Darcy puzzled out Mr. Collins's incoherent sentence, wondering if the man had graduated from the seminary.

"I had not expected to meet one of her ladyship's illustrious relations in such a place as this." Mr. Collins offered a low bow, his hands extended out to the side. "I greet you, Mr. Darcy, and offer you the intelligence of your aunt's condition. Lady Catherine was in excellent health when I last saw her only four days ago."

"That is good news, Mr. Collins," said Darcy. "I would have expected nothing less, for my aunt has always spoken of how her constitution is so strong that she is never ill."

The man nodded so rapidly that Darcy thought he might disconnect his head from his shoulders. "She has made the same observation to me on multiple occasions."

A thought seemed to strike Mr. Collins, and he glanced between Miss Elizabeth and Darcy several times, apparently trying to make sense of something. Then he turned his attention to Miss Elizabeth.

"A thousand apologies, Cousin Elizabeth, but is Mr. Darcy the man of whom your father spoke?"

"As I was not present for your conversation," said Miss Elizabeth, laughter in her voice, "I cannot say."

"Oh, I beg your pardon," said he, not realizing he had just apologized. "Your father informed me there was a young man new to the neighborhood paying court to you. Am I correct in apprehending that is Mr. Darcy?"

Miss Elizabeth shifted uncomfortably. When she glanced at him, Darcy smiled, attempting to convey to her that Mr. Collins had not offended him. Relieved, she answered her cousin:

"I would not call it a courtship, Mr. Collins, nor do I think my father meant to convey it in such terms."

"Yes, Mr. Bennet is correct," Darcy hastened to say, drawing her eyes to him. "Nothing is yet decided, but I am intrigued by Miss Elizabeth and have every intention of following my interest to its natural conclusion, should we mutually agree upon it."

Miss Elizabeth's response was by no means disappointing, though it was rather more closed than was her wont. She said nothing, but she regarded him with an earnestness he thought boded well for his future intentions.

"Ah, then that is excellent, Mr. Darcy, for I am of the firmest opinion that my cousins are excellent ladies."

Darcy turned back to the parson to see him regarding them, his smile nearly beatific.

"It is fortunate that you are in a position where you may take advantage of your acquaintance with Cousin Elizabeth. Should your cousin, Miss Anne de Bourgh still be among the living, that avenue would not be open to you."

The comment stunned the entire company to silence. Miss Elizabeth regarded the parson with concealed hilarity, while her elder sister regarded him with horror. Miss Kitty appeared uncertain, while Miss Mary, curiously, looked on him with satisfaction mixed with relief. For Darcy's part, could not decide whether to laugh at the man's absurdity or take him to task.

"Are you suggesting, Mr. Collins," said Darcy at length after considering his reply, "that it is *fortunate* that my cousin is deceased?"

Such a look of terror came over the parson's countenance that Darcy almost pitied the man.

"A thousand apologizes, Mr. Darcy!" cried he. "A thousand times a thousand! That was certainly not my intention at all!"

"Nor did I think it was," said Darcy, taking pity on the man. "I understand your meaning and will only state that I am a fortunate man, indeed. Or I will be if I can provoke the sort of regard in Miss Elizabeth that I have for her."

Mr. Collins bowed low several times, then he turned back to Miss Lucas to remove himself from Darcy's notice. The others turned back to their discourse, and Darcy allowed himself to regard Miss Elizabeth again. The woman faced him, her lips contorted to refrain from laughing aloud. When Darcy quirked an eyebrow at her, she lost her countenance, though she restrained her merriment to a few low chuckles.

"I believe my father told you something of his suspicions of his cousin?"

It was a challenge, one Darcy was happy to accept. "He did. And he appears to have been proven correct."

Though Miss Elizabeth nodded, she appeared distracted. "Did you mean what you said?"

"About such matters, I never dissemble, Miss Elizabeth. Now, shall we return to Longbourn?"

She assented, accepting his arm with a rush of color in her cheeks. Darcy was content. Perhaps he had not intended to speak in such a forthright fashion so quickly. But he could not repent of it. On the contrary, he wished her to know of his seriousness without the possibility of misinterpretation.

When Elizabeth met Mr. Darcy two days later, it was with some measure of excitement. She had seen him the previous day also when he and Mr. Bingley had visited Longbourn, and even her father had commented on the alteration in the gentleman's manner. Gone was the friendly yet reserved man they had come to know; in his place was a man who had no reservation, who approached her with unmistakable interest in a woman. The prospect both frightened and exhilarated Elizabeth, such that her feelings were a jumble of confused cacophony, an unfathomable mixture of anticipation and longing.

"Miss Elizabeth," said he, swinging down from his horse in front of her on the path she walked. "How fortunate that I have found you at last."

"At last?" echoed Elizabeth unconsciously. "I do not understand — you visited yesterday."

The gentleman gave her a wry grin. "Yes, I did. But I have ridden out every morning this week hoping to encounter you during your walks, and this is the first time I have been fortunate enough to find you."

For a moment, Elizabeth considered calling him out for embellishing. Then she realized he spoke nothing less than the truth. Somehow, he had sought her out before he even knew he wished to deepen their connection.

"For what purpose, Mr. Darcy?" asked she, falling back on her typical playful riposte. "If we were discovered walking alone in this fashion, our reputations might be affected."

"Were we in some secluded location, perhaps you might be correct," replied Mr. Darcy. "But on a path in view of anyone who should pass us by? I am afraid I must disagree with you on that score.

"However," continued he before Elizabeth could muster a response, "I would have you know that if it should come to pass as you suggest, I am not a man who will refuse to uphold his obligations. It would not be an obligation so much as a privilege."

"You have suddenly become bold!" exclaimed Elizabeth, feeling off-balance.

"I merely understand what I want." The man's look was a caress. "Now that I have identified it, I mean to let no one other than you to stand in my way."

Elizabeth found herself unable to respond. When his look suddenly lightened and he changed the subject, she could not but feel gratitude.

"Were you walking anywhere in particular, or just meandering about the estate?"

Elizabeth gave the man an arch look, feeling her control returning.

"That shows you still have much to learn of me, Mr. Darcy. I do not meander."

"Then where are you bound?" asked the gentleman.

"To the prominence to the north of my father's estate," said Elizabeth, motioning past the gentleman. "It is two miles away and I do not follow the path often. But occasionally I find myself desirous of the view, which is quite fine."

"If you will have me, I should like to accompany you."

Nodding shyly, Elizabeth accepted his arm, and they turned toward the hill, the reins to his stallion held loosely in his other hand. For a time, they said nothing, for Mr. Darcy appeared contemplative, while Elizabeth was still gathering the threads of her composure. Then a thought came to her, and she turned to him.

"I apologize if it is inappropriate, Mr. Darcy, but I have a question." The gentleman's inquisitive look gave Elizabeth all the impetus to respond. "Mr. Collins mentioned something about your cousin and your aunt?"

The exasperation in the gentleman's countenance reminded her of the parson's faux pas, but he did not direct it at her. "My aunt long wished for a union between myself and her daughter, claiming she had agreed to it with her sister, my mother. Yet my mother said nothing to me of the matter, and my father did not give any credence to Lady Catherine's words."

"Then you did not consider yourself bound to the agreement?"

"Not at all," replied Mr. Darcy. "My cousin passed away two years ago, and while I visited her every spring while her daughter yet lived, Lady Catherine has preferred my uncle's company in recent years." Mr. Darcy shrugged. "I can only assume my presence reminds her of what she has lost."

Elizabeth nodded, but she did not prolong the discussion. They spoke of more commonplace subjects as they walked, the sort of unimportant commentary prevalent between two people who were, by now, well acquainted and comfortable in each other's company. The place where Elizabeth had met Mr. Darcy was more than half of the way to the hill, and before long they were climbing its lower slopes, intent upon reaching the summit above.

When they stepped onto the hill's crown, Elizabeth looked out over the landscape so familiar and loved, pointing out the various features to the gentleman. The hill was not a tall one, but it was the tallest in the vicinity, rendering the view from its summit a fine one on most sides where woods did not impede the view. From the crest, they could easily see the house at Netherfield in the distance, and while Longbourn was hidden in the foliage, Elizabeth could easily pick out its location and could see the steeple of Longbourn church rising like a sentry over the sea of the surrounding forest.

"I love this view, Mr. Darcy," said she, sighing with pleasure, the vistas spread out over her seeming to encompass all the world. "My father showed me this place when I was fifteen, and since then I have often come here when weather and circumstances permitted. To a man worldly and well-traveled it may seem of little enough importance, but I have rarely ventured past London, and have not traveled at all to the north. To my current understanding, this is the dearest place I know."

"On the contrary, Miss Elizabeth," said Mr. Darcy, his voice husky with some emotion, "I have rarely seen a lovelier view than this."

Something informed Elizabeth that if she looked at him, she would find herself unbearably embarrassed. As such, she kept her gaze fixed on the rolling hills and groves, the fields and paths, the bounty before her as familiar as her hand.

"Are there any other wonders in the vicinity you might show me?"

Elizabeth chuckled. "There are a few. I usually only go as far as my legs can carry me, but I *can* ride. When I wish it, I ride out to a small valley with a stream around the east side of this hill. It is a picturesque scene. But I should not speak of such things to you, for a man who lives near the peaks must be accustomed to wonder and find such poor offerings as my home insufficient fare."

"There *are* wonders aplenty near my home," replied Mr. Darcy. "Someday I should like to show them to you."

His tone and his inference combined to pull Elizabeth's eyes to his face at last. While Mr. Darcy copied her in looking out over the land below them, Elizabeth saw that half of his attention or more was on her, the admiration contained in his look beyond anything he had yet displayed. For the first time, the fluttering of love stirred within her heart, fanned by the flames of his obvious appreciation. For a long moment, she found she could not respond, and he did not speak to fill the silence.

At length, Elizabeth said: "I believe I should like to see them someday, Mr. Darcy." A sudden thought crossed her mind. "Though I know it is probably not known to you, have you ever heard of a town called Lambton?"

Surprise crossed Mr. Darcy's countenance. "Lambton is not five miles from Pemberley, Miss Elizabeth. Did you hear the name from my companions?" He grinned and added: "Miss Bingley speaks in blandishments about the wonders of my home and its locale, but when she stayed at Pemberley, she did not bestir herself beyond the edge of the formal gardens behind the house. To Lambton, she was perfectly indifferent, so I cannot imagine she spoke of it."

"No, I have heard no whisper of it from any of your companions. It is a surprising coincidence, Mr. Darcy, for my aunt spent some years of her life as a child living in Lambton."

"That *is* odd, indeed," replied Mr. Darcy. "Now I am eager to meet your aunt, for we may know some of the same people."

"I am sure she would be happy to make your acquaintance, for you may offer her newer intelligence of the town."

"It should please me to offer it," agreed Mr. Darcy. "If your aunt wishes to return to visit the neighborhood, perhaps she would consent to stay at Pemberley."

Elizabeth demurred. "I am certain they would not feel comfortable staying when they are not much acquainted with those who live there."

"You forget something, Miss Elizabeth. In time, one may live there who is intimately acquainted with them."

The inference stunned and thrilled Elizabeth, such that she could not remove her eyes from him. Amid the glory of nature among the stones of the place she loved as much as any in the world, Elizabeth's eyes opened to the possibility of her future. It was a bright future, indeed.

Chapter IX

*P*reparations for the ball were proceeding, and the time had come to dispatch the invitations to the local gentlemen. Bingley had also issued a general invitation to the officers of the regiment, an excellent notion, Darcy thought, given what he had witnessed at the assembly, where the number of ladies had far exceeded the gentlemen. While Darcy thought little about the officers, had nothing in common with them, and was not interested in much association with them, their addition could only enhance Bingley's ball. Providing for his guests' enjoyment was, after all, Bingley's responsibility, and additional dance partners would do so admirably.

The way Miss Bingley carried on as the evening's arrangements took shape, Darcy might have thought she was planning a ball in which she expected the queen's attendance at least. It was all for him — Darcy knew this, for the woman appeared to watch him every time she announced something, every arrangement she chose. Darcy could well withstand her attempts to provoke his approval. That his lack of response annoyed her did not bother him in the slightest.

"There," said Miss Bingley five days before the ball. "The invitations are complete."

"Then I shall summon the butler and entrust them to his care," said

Bingley. "He may dispatch the footmen to the homes of our neighbors."

Miss Bingley nodded but did not appear to care. As was her wont, she turned to Darcy, a coy smile fixed on him. "We shall have an evening far finer than anything these *people* have any right to expect."

There was no reason to respond, and Darcy did not, instead watching Bingley who was searching through the invitations, his brows lowered in concentration. Then he grinned and plucked one from the pile, nodding with satisfaction.

"Ah, here it is," said he.

Miss Bingley regarded her brother with open confusion. "What are you doing, Charles? Those invitations must be delivered at once if we are to have anyone to host."

"I understand that, Caroline," said Bingley, ringing the bell.

When the housekeeper entered, he handed her the invitations, instructing her to see them to the butler and their ultimate dispositions. The invitation he had plucked from the rest he still held in his hand. The housekeeper noted it, but she did not question his purpose. Instead, she accepted the pile and made her way from the room. By this time, Miss Bingley was cross with impatience.

"What are you doing, Charles? Is there someone in this place who has earned even *your* enmity? Regardless of what they have done, it would not be proper to single them out for exclusion."

"Not at all," said Bingley. "This invitation is for the Bennets; I mean to deliver it to them in person."

In an instant, Miss Bingley traversed the divide between perplexed exasperation and fury. "Charles!" snapped she. "That is not proper!"

"It is eminently proper," retorted he. "We may deliver them all if we wish, though it is not usually done. With the Bennets, our friendship has grown so much that I wish to ensure, with no misunderstanding, how much I esteem them."

"You cannot possibly be considering Miss Bennet for a wife!" cried Miss Bingley, voicing the fear that had gnawed at her these past weeks.

"At present, I am not so far gone," was Bingley's calm reply. "But that does not signify."

Miss Bingley gave him a mutinous glare, one Bingley had no trouble withstanding.

"Nothing you say will alter my purpose, Caroline. I am quite resolved."

This was how Darcy found himself in a carriage with Bingley and his sister—the Hursts remained at Netherfield—less than two hours later. Miss Bingley did not accept her defeat with any grace, her aggrieved looks at her brother and more pleading ones at Darcy speaking to her disgruntlement. Both men ignored her cheerfully, and the carriage rolled on to its destination.

The Bennets had gathered in the sitting-room when Darcy entered, but while he observed this, he only had eyes for Miss Elizabeth. With her sisters, she rose and curtseyed to welcome them, her eyes finding Darcy's as if his companions did not exist. An understanding seemed to pass between them, she was content with his obvious regard while Darcy ached for more. The greetings exchanged, and the welcomes offered, Darcy accepted a seat next to Miss Elizabeth, hardly conscious of anything else in the room. Now that the opportunity had presented itself, Darcy meant to take full advantage of it.

"Miss Bennet, Mr. Bennet," said Bingley a moment later. "My sister, my friend, and I have come for a particular purpose this morning."

Bingley brandished the invitation like a bouquet for a special woman and passed it to Miss Bennet, his manner suggesting that while the invitation was for them all, Miss Bennet was the only member of the family in his thoughts. It was so much like Darcy was behaving with Miss Elizabeth that he fought to stifle a laugh. Miss Elizabeth, ever perceptive, understood him at once and covered her mouth, her eyes dancing with merriment.

"On Tuesday next," continued Bingley, again speaking directly to Miss Bennet, "my sisters and I have planned to host a ball. It would please me very much if you and your family will consent to join us."

"Of course, Mr. Bingley," said Miss Bennet. "We are delighted to accept."

Bingley gave her a great beaming smile, but the right of response belonged to Mr. Bennet. "Indeed, with such displays as this, I doubt I could keep my daughters away from the amusement, even if I locked them in their rooms."

While Bingley nodded, Mr. Bennet's eyes turned to Darcy, a searching quality inherent in his gaze. Darcy met the man's concern, held his gaze, then gave him a slight nod in answer to his unasked question. For a moment, Bennet studied him. Then his face creased with a grin, and he nodded in acknowledgment or thanks.

"Is Mr. Collins about?" asked Bingley, pulling Darcy's attention away from Bennet. "The invitation includes your cousin, for I did not think it necessary to provide him with a separate invitation."

"My cousin has been absent often these past days," said Bennet, appearing for all the world like he knew something the rest of the company did not. "He is presently visiting Lucas Lodge. But we shall be certain to convey your solicitations to him when he returns."

With a nod, apparently satisfied, Bingley turned his full attention on Miss Bennet. Taking it as his cue, Darcy did the same with Miss Elizabeth, barely noticing that Miss Bingley was trying to gain his attention. No doubt she wished to depart at once. Darcy did not agree, and he ignored her as if she did not exist.

"Was your cousin's purpose not to extend an olive branch to you all?" asked Darcy.

Miss Elizabeth nodded. "It was. But now that he has offered it, Lucas Lodge appears curiously more agreeable to him than Longbourn."

It was simple conjecture to deduce why that was so, but he refrained, not wishing to speak of Collins. For some moments, they spoke softly together, while Darcy attempted to find some way to introduce what he truly wished to discuss with her. In the back of his mind and the edges of his vision, he noted how Miss Bingley wavered between the desire to interfere with her brother's attention toward Miss Bennet and Darcy's with Miss Elizabeth. Because of her dithering, she accomplished neither objective, her dissatisfaction manifesting itself in continual expressions of a desire to depart.

This went on for some moments, which led Darcy to forget that Miss Bingley even existed, so focused was he on his conversation with Miss Elizabeth. How long they had sat there, he could not say, though long enough to anger Miss Bingley so much that her usual barely concealed hostility frayed into open spite. How it all came about, Darcy could not say, for he had no notion of anything other than Miss Elizabeth, but at length that composure snapped.

"I am certain *you* think so, Miss Mary," the woman's sneering voice rose over the company, audible to all. "But we are more discerning than that. Perhaps you should focus on those narrow subjects you can comprehend instead of those matters of which you have no notion."

Before anyone could respond to her rudeness, the youngest Bennet's voice rose in response. "If you intend to ridicule and behave like a vile shrew, I wonder why you come at all."

"Kitty!" cried Miss Bennet, stifling her sister's outburst.

Miss Bingley drew in a breath for a retort, but her brother stood and silenced her with a sharp glare.

"That is enough, Caroline."

Without regard to his sister, who stared at him with incomprehension and growing anger, Bingley turned to Jane.

"Perhaps we have stayed too long today, for there is much yet to be done. Your sister may have spoken out of turn, but you must remember that *mine* provoked her."

Miss Bingley's anger turned to pure fury, but Bingley did not notice. "Thank you for a wonderful visit, Miss Bennet, but we must depart."

As one the company stood, Miss Bingley clearly eager to be gone, while Bingley was reluctant. Darcy himself did not wish to leave, but he knew his friend had the right of it. Yet he had not yet made his communication to Miss Elizabeth!

The Bennets agreed graciously, and the whole party made their way from the sitting-room toward the vestibule, Miss Bingley eagerly in the lead, as if she could not wait to wash the dust of this place from her feet. Darcy hung back with Miss Elizabeth, allowing the others to take the lead. Bennet made some jesting comment to him, but Darcy hardly heard him, intensely focused as he was on the woman by his side and the question he meant to ask her. When they reached the entrance and the others began making their way outside, Darcy seized his opportunity.

"Miss Elizabeth," said he, pulling her attention to him. "Might I request your first sets at Bingley's ball?"

At first confused, her gaze softened, and she nodded. "You may, Mr. Darcy. I should be happy to cede them to you."

The tension extinguished, Darcy looked at her with gratitude, bringing her hand to his lips. "Thank you, Miss Elizabeth. I shall anticipate them breathlessly."

It was, perhaps, a little silly, but the irrational part of him hoped no one had noticed their slight tardiness in exiting the house. Such hopes were to be dashed, however, the moment they emerged, as an incensed Miss Bingley confronted them. To Darcy, she appeared to blame him, as if he had betrayed her in some fashion. To Miss Elizabeth, however, she appeared ready to extend talons and fight for her prey, rending flesh to stake her claim. Elizabeth calmly regarded her, cool disdain upon unconcern. Then she turned away and looked at Darcy.

"Thank you, Mr. Darcy. I shall see you at the ball if our paths do not cross again before."

"Do not doubt they will, Miss Elizabeth," replied he, taking his cue from her and avoiding Miss Bingley. "If I must go five days without your company, all the light will retreat from the world."

Miss Elizabeth chuckled and curtseyed to his bow. Darcy, having kissed her hand inside, refrained from doing so in front of Miss

Bingley, though he was sorely tempted, if only to further pierce the unpleasant woman's conceit. Seeing something of his sister's state of mind, Bingley arrived to collect her, and he directed her to the carriage, nothing of hesitance in his manner. A few moments later, the carriage lurched into motion for the interminably short journey back to Netherfield.

A part of Darcy remained aware of his companions, how Bingley berated his sister for her words to the younger Bennet sisters. The way Miss Bingley ignored her brother, peering at Darcy himself, also did not escape his attention. With his open display to Miss Elizabeth, there was no possibility of concealment any longer; Miss Bingley now knew with no hint of doubt what Darcy's feelings were, and he did not care to continue to deny it. The confrontation he had avoided since coming to Hertfordshire was at hand, and he would not shirk from making his sentiments known to her.

"Brother!" spat Miss Bingley when they had reached the estate. "This madness had gone on too far. You have tied us to this insignificant speck with this ball you have contrived as if anyone here would understand culture if we served it to them on a platter. But enough is enough. After the ball, we *must* go to London and never return."

"You may go if you wish," replied Bingley, unaffected by her displeasure. "But I am fixed at Netherfield. The Hursts may accompany you if you wish."

"That is unacceptable!" She glared at him, wild with fury and desperation. "What has come over you? Are the Bennets witches, that they have ensorcelled you, hedged you about with mazes of the mind, intent upon destroying your good sense? They are nothing! Any connection with them will only bring about the acutest misery!"

"And yet, I have no intention of departing."

"Yes, you will!" screeched Miss Bingley. "Jane Bennet is in no way suitable. She has nothing. She *is* nothing. We shall be the laughingstock of society should you lose all sense of yourself and offer for her.

"And as for Miss Elizabeth," spat Miss Bingley, turning to Darcy, "you must be mad to even consider her. What is she but a hoyden, a woman grasping and artful? Do you not remember yourself, your heritage, your very position in society?"

"I remember all these things, Miss Bingley," replied Darcy, maintaining an even tone. "An alliance with Miss Elizabeth would betray none of them."

"You have all gone mad! This is insanity. Perhaps I should petition your uncle to commit you to Bedlam!"

"He would laugh in your face, Miss Bingley," said Darcy. "*If* you could even gain an audience with him. Let us not speak around the subject; I know what you want, and I am not inclined to give it to you."

Miss Bingley regarded him, her face a mass of conflicting emotions. "My education is from the finest seminaries; I possess all the accomplishments necessary to be an excellent wife."

"To someone who values such things, you do." Darcy stared holes into her, willing her to understand and desist. "I have never had any interest in you, Miss Bingley. You have spent two years trying to induce me to notice you. Well, you have been successful. I *have* noticed. But still, I have no interest."

"You must!" wailed the woman.

"Bingley, are you certain you should not institutionalize your sister? It appears the madness is all on her part."

"Trust me, Darcy," replied Bingley, glaring at his sister. "I am tempted beyond measure."

"Miss Bingley," said Darcy before the woman could speak again. "I do not wish to have you for a wife. Do you not think I would have requested your hand or even behaved as a suitor if I did? I do not even *like* you. You are everything wrong with society to me: grasping, artful, contemptuous, mean, callous, and shrewish. Can I make myself any plainer than this?"

For a moment, Darcy thought she might respond. Even a physical response was not out of the question, so infuriated had she become. Then without warning, she whirled and stalked away, her gaze flaying the servants where they scurried from her path. A moment later, she was gone, leaving silence in her wake.

"I had not expected her to capitulate that easily," murmured Bingley, staring at the place where she had gone.

"She has not yet given up," said Darcy.

Bingley nodded. "Against all sanity, it appears. Yet her cause is doomed, even if she will not confess it." Then he turned to Darcy. "I apologize for my sister's behavior."

"And I apologize for the way I spoke to her."

"Nonsense," replied Bingley, his tone clipped. "It appears Caroline needed to hear it. After the ball, I might ask Hurst to take her to town. Or I may send a letter to my family in the north; she could stay with one of my uncles for a time. Caroline will not like it, but I no longer care what she likes."

Darcy nodded, but his mind was considering other paths. Perhaps

Bingley did not wish to confront his sister's depravity, or perhaps he remained convinced she would not act in defiance of all good sense. Darcy knew better. The woman who had just departed had shown in word and deed her willingness to go to the ends of extremity to secure what she wanted, what she felt she deserved. Darcy would put nothing past her.

It was not until later that Darcy learned how correct he was. The afternoon was a tense cloud of suspicion and anger, moiling affront and calculation. For a wonder, Miss Bingley said little—or it was correct to say that few words issued from her mouth, for she was engaged in watching him. While she said nothing, her eyes spoke in language more eloquent than words, their meaning clear in her desire to do whatever it took to ensure she attained the prize at his expense.

This state of affairs remained through dinner and thereafter. Miss Bingley retired early that evening, much to the surprise of all. Mrs. Hurst, who had watched her sister all afternoon and into the evening, shrank with relief when Miss Bingley was gone. It was not long before she too retired, leaving the three men together. With the ladies departed, Bingley rose and went to the sideboard, pouring three generous measures of brandy, passing one to Hurst and the other to Darcy. Though he felt like flinging the entire contents back against his throat, wished to relish the burn as it made its way down his throat, Darcy steeled himself to take measured sips.

"You have set the cat amongst the pigeons now," said Hurst, draining his glass with less restraint than Darcy, then rising to pour himself more. "My gratitude at missing this afternoon's unpleasantness, I cannot find words to state, but I have heard of it from my wife."

Darcy regarded him with interest; he did not remember seeing Mrs. Hurst while arguing with the woman's sister.

"I suppose I need not inform you that you must take care," said he, gesturing with his glass at Darcy.

"Not at all," replied Darcy, sipping again at his drink.

"What are you saying, Hurst?" asked Bingley, apparently surprised.

"Do not be foolish, Bingley," growled Hurst. "Your sister is not a woman to be gainsaid, especially in the matter of her ambitions. She will try to force Darcy's hand—mark my words."

Bingley appeared to flounder, so Darcy stepped into the breach. "Whether Miss Bingley will try something, I know not."

It was nothing less than a lie, but Darcy did not wish to cause his friend any more grief.

"But I am not unprepared. Do not concern yourself for me."

Hurst gave him a slow nod. "I cannot imagine you would not be ready for her."

"I am prepared," said Darcy, nodding in Hurst's direction. "But know this: I shall not bow to whatever Miss Bingley contrives. She may put herself in my bed with all Meryton to see, and I will not relent."

"If Caroline understood that, she *might* desist."

"I can inform her if you wish."

Hurst looked at him for a long moment, then shook his head. "It will do no good. She will not listen."

"No, I cannot imagine she would," interjected Bingley. He directed a pleading look at Darcy. "I hope this will not end our friendship, Darcy."

"Of course not, Bingley," replied Darcy. "I know you have nothing to do with your sister's intrigues. Do not concern yourself, for I am not without resources."

Bingley appeared relieved. "Once the ball is over, I shall take Caroline to the north myself. If Hurst and Louisa remain here, you can stay with them. Otherwise, you must interrupt your courting while I am away."

"That is acceptable, Bingley. If you want my advice, you may wish to search for a husband for your sister, present it to her as a fait accompli. She reaches too high."

"She is likely to be burned by it," muttered Bingley.

Agreement was certain, but Darcy did not feel there was anything to be gained by belaboring the point. Only a few moments later, the three men departed the room to seek their beds. Perhaps the following morning would bring a new perspective, though Darcy knew they would gain nothing if Miss Bingley did not gain this insight. When he arrived at his room, a surprise awaited him.

"Snell?" asked Darcy, noting a cot situated no more than five paces in front of the door to his bedchamber. "Do you propose to defend me with your very life?"

Darcy had intended it to be a jest, but his manservant, as was his wont, saw no humor in anything. "If I must, Mr. Darcy. I speak on behalf of all your servants, as you recall."

"I do," said Darcy with a chuckle. "But I had not expected this."

"You would understand if you knew the truth of it."

Darcy eyed his man. "Has something happened since I spoke to you this afternoon?"

The man's countenance remained grim. "After leaving your argument, I learned Miss Bingley approached Mrs. Nichols and demanded the keys to the estate. As she is the mistress, the housekeeper had no choice but to hand them to her."

Darcy understood the implications at once; but Snell had not finished his explanation.

"In response, I approached the housekeeper when Miss Bingley retired for the evening, doing so when they were speaking together. I requested a cot to be delivered to your rooms at once."

Concern turning to mirth, Darcy wondered at the audacity of his man. "Might I suppose Miss Bingley did not appreciate your demand?"

Snell's lips twisted into the nearest approximation of wryness that Darcy had ever seen. "Appreciation? No, that is impossible. The beauty of the situation is that she could not protest without revealing her interest in the matter. Then I explained to the housekeeper exactly where I wished her to place the cot."

Darcy could not hold in his mirth. "Snell, you are a treasure!"

"Miss Bingley," said Snell, ignoring his master's chortles, "appeared none too pleased to learn that any attempt she made on *you* must first bypass *me*, but she made no protest. By now, I expect she is pacing her room in her most revealing negligee, gnashing her teeth in frustration at the impossibility of her designs."

"Good man," said Darcy, placing his hand on Snell's shoulder. "Do you require additional blankets? That cot does not appear comfortable."

"This meets my needs, Mr. Darcy," said he. "I would rather endure a few uncomfortable nights than endure Miss Bingley as the mistress of your estate."

"I understand you completely, Snell. Nothing would horrify me more than to wake up tomorrow morning and know that I am shackled to Miss Bingley forever."

Snell nodded and gave a slight bow and went about a few tasks while Darcy prepared to retire. The question was, Darcy considered as he lay in his bed a short time later, whether he should alert Bingley to what Snell had discovered. Mild-mannered man though he was, Darcy could well imagine Bingley's reaction, his disgust for his sister's conniving ways.

Two reasons forced any such consideration from Darcy's mind. The first was that he could handle Miss Bingley and resist any attempt she might make. The second was that Bingley was preparing to host a ball for the neighborhood. Should Miss Bingley enact her machinations now, it might force Bingley to postpone or cancel his ball to deal with his sister, resulting in some loss of standing with his neighbors. Now that Snell had thwarted Miss Bingley, for the short term at least, Darcy was loath to interrupt his friend's designs.

No, it was better to restrain himself, to remain watchful and trust Snell to frustrate any thought Miss Bingley might have through such means as entering his room at night. During the days, Darcy would exercise his own form of vigilance, ensuring Miss Bingley had no opportunity to try anything with him.

Besides, if Miss Bingley succeeded, he would refuse her, as he had already determined. It may cause some small measure of scandal for Bingley, but he thought those in the neighborhood, already inclined to disapprove of his sister, would not blame him for her weakness.

With that thought, Darcy surrendered himself to sleep, trusting Snell to keep any night phantasms away from him.

CHAPTER X

*B*y the time the Bennet family arrived at Netherfield the night of the ball, Elizabeth was bursting with anticipation. The day after she had last met Mr. Darcy, the rains had descended on Hertfordshire, rendering the landscape a sodden mess, one not fit for anyone to be out of doors. Denied her walks and bereft of Mr. Darcy's company, she spent those days trying to maintain an even temper, often gazing out the windows at the sheets of rain, wondering how she would ever endure.

The Longbourn family arrived at Netherfield punctual to their time and made their way through the family greeting line, but Elizabeth noted none of it. Mr. Bingley's effusive welcomes and Caroline Bingley's acid stares could do nothing to hold her attention, for she had no interest in anyone other than Mr. Darcy.

When she finally saw him in the ballroom upon stepping inside, her heart swelled, near to bursting in her breast. Some indefinable sense must have told him that she entered, for the moment she espied him the gentlemen turned and caught sight of her, wasting no time before approaching and greeting her, his gaze on her a smoldering inferno, hinting at pleasures and sensations she could not quite understand.

"Miss Elizabeth," said he, grasping her hand to press a lingering kiss to it. "How happy I am to see you."

"As I am to see you," replied Elizabeth automatically. Every response to Mr. Darcy's overtures was instinctual as if it was meant to be. "I hope you have been well these past days."

"I have endured them as best I could," replied Mr. Darcy. The gentleman drew in close, and in a low voice said: "Are you prepared to dance, Miss Elizabeth?"

"As one usually is," laughed Elizabeth. "Perhaps you did not know, sir, but I have always been accounted a social woman. I have never had difficulty attracting dance partners."

"That is unfortunate, Miss Elizabeth. If I asked you to dance only with me tonight, would you agree?"

"I doubt you could say anything to induce me to agree to so unreasonable a request."

The gentleman sighed, and Elizabeth was not certain his regret was feigned. "Then I suppose I must give a good account of myself, for if I do not, I must stand by the side of the floor, watching as other men take you away from me repeatedly, all the while wishing I was in their shoes until their dance ends."

"That would be for the best, sir," said Elizabeth, holding her laughter in with a force of will. "We would not wish you to become surly, for it would not do to offend Mr. Bingley's neighbors."

The man fixed her with a wry smile. "No, Miss Elizabeth, it would not. I shall allow others to carry *that* particular standard."

With that, their conversation became more serious and less playful. They spoke of the arrangements — which Elizabeth could confess were quite fine, proving Miss Bingley was an adept hostess. They spoke of their expectations for the evening and what lay beyond, Mr. Darcy informing her of recent events, that he had no wish to leave Netherfield, regardless of his difficulties with its mistress. He also informed her of the possibility of Miss Bingley going to the north and his friend's need to go to town, though he assured her that Bingley had no more desire to be long absent from Longbourn than he had himself.

"I know not what it concerns," said Mr. Darcy when Elizabeth asked him, "for Bingley has not vouchsafed the nature of his business to me. All he said is that he must go for a few days, perhaps as many as five."

"What shall you do in the meantime, sir?" asked Elizabeth, showing him an arch grin. "If staying in a house with Miss Bingley is uncomfortable for you now, I cannot imagine that it will be anything other than immeasurably worse when he is gone."

"That is true," replied Mr. Darcy. "I have not consulted with my friend yet, but I had thought I might accompany him and return when he does." Mr. Darcy grinned at her, adding: "Bingley has suggested he might send his sister to the north. If Miss Bingley refuses to go, there may be another way to dispense with her company. Should we both go to town, Miss Bingley would doubtlessly take the opportunity to follow thereafter, hoping to persuade us against returning. Should she do that, it may be possible to leave her in London while we return."

Elizabeth laughed and wagged a finger at him. "That is devious, Mr. Darcy, to manipulate Miss Bingley in such a way."

"I said nothing of encouraging her or even mentioning such a course," protested the man, though his eyes shone with mirth. "I am familiar enough with Miss Bingley's character that I believe I can predict her actions."

"While there are certain drawbacks to her absence, I cannot imagine you would both not be more comfortable alone."

"Indeed," replied Darcy.

The gentleman fell silent for a moment, his manner faintly searching, as if trying to determine what he should do. Or, given the way he regarded her, Elizabeth felt it possible he considered how she would react to something he wished to tell her. The truth became known to her at once, for he did not wait long.

"Should I return to London," said he, speaking slowly, "I have thought of asking my sister if she wishes to accompany me back to Netherfield." A sense of wryness fell over him as he added: "Then again, should Miss Bingley learn of it, her return to Hertfordshire will become doubly imperative in her own mind."

Elizabeth nodded, knowing he spoke the truth. "Then you must take care to ensure she remains ignorant of it." Regarding him for a long moment, trying to take his measure, Elizabeth said: "Do you suppose your sister will wish to return with you?"

"Georgiana gets on well with Bingley, and if I assure her of Miss Bingley's absence, she will not object. Furthermore, I have made several mentions of a *certain lady* in my correspondence, and I believe she wishes to make her acquaintance."

"Oh," said Elizabeth, not quite understanding what she should say. "What sort of girl is your sister?"

"Very shy," replied Mr. Darcy. "There have been few ladies her age with whom she could become friends."

"She is sixteen?" At Mr. Darcy's nod, Elizabeth said: "Then she is a little younger than Kitty. Perhaps my sister would enjoy making her acquaintance. We should all like to meet her."

"Then we shall call it settled," said Mr. Darcy as if he had been waiting for a sign that bringing his sister to the neighborhood was welcome.

A moment later the music for the first dance rang out over the company. Mr. Darcy turned to Elizabeth and gave her a questioning look, to which she smiled, hiding the fluttering of her heart, and put her hand in his. They joined the line forming on the dance floor, their focus entirely on each other, no other considerations intruding on the burgeoning passion between them.

Elizabeth and Darcy noticed nothing of any interest or scrutiny they drew from the rest of the company, but that did not mean there was none. Those who knew Elizabeth best, having had the pleasure of her company all their lives, looked on with interest and pleasure. Not all the attention they drew was pleased, or even benign. One at least looked on with utter contempt, anger, and even determination. That lady made no attempt to disguise her growing rage and frustration. To one who paid little attention to such things, Bennet supposed they might not readily understand. He did not fail to observe his surroundings; Miss Bingley's feelings were clear.

It was a little enough thing, he thought, this business of understanding Miss Caroline Bingley. One reason he did not like town and refused to go often was how artificial he found them, how each person played a part, and those parts most often disguised depravity to which he did not wish to expose himself and his family. The so-called highest tier of society was nothing more than a collection of fools, in his opinion, congratulating themselves on their superiority with no true justification.

Miss Bingley was amusing, as she had no right to hold herself higher than Bennet and his neighbors, not even the thin rationalizations used by those of society. The woman spent her life attempting to flee from the truth of her background. It was more than diverting—it was nothing less than pathetic. To induce her to understanding, however, was impossible, and he had long determined to take his mirth where he could and move on.

This instance, however, was unlike others, in that Elizabeth's—and possibly Jane's—happiness was at stake. It had long been a source of amusement that many in the neighborhood—chief among them his wife's obnoxious sister—accused him of absence from his daughters' affairs, a lackadaisical parenting style that left them open to misbehavior and ridicule. Bennet could well own to being unwilling to involve himself, preferring to allow his daughters to manage their problems and come to him when necessary, but he was not blind. Jane and Elizabeth were such good girls, with excellent demeanors, and he had long allowed them to take the lead with their younger sisters.

In the matter of Elizabeth's happiness, there was little Bennet would not do, and that was equally true for any of his other daughters. Miss Bingley, he knew, was a threat, so focused was she on Darcy. Thus, Bennet watched the woman as she seethed and plotted, unless he missed his guess. When the woman drew close to him, he took the opportunity to have words with her.

"You would do well to let it go."

For a moment, he thought Miss Bingley had not heard him—that, or the woman ignored him. Either was possible. He opened his mouth to speak again when she turned to regard him.

"I know not of what you speak."

Bennet chuckled and shook his head. "On the contrary, Miss Bingley, I am assured that you know exactly what I am saying. No one with even a hint of sense can misunderstand your plotting against your brother's friend."

Miss Bingley's gaze might have scalded molten lava. "It is typical among your class to assume your cleverness exceeds the reality of your squalor."

"*My* class?" asked Bennet, diverted at her conceit. "A gentleman's class, you mean. I apologize, Miss Bingley, for I have no thought to offend, but I had no notion that the daughter of a tradesman understood such matters."

Insulted beyond measure, the woman spat: "I have been educated at—"

"That is irrelevant, and you know it," interrupted Bennet, "little though you wish to acknowledge the truth. To some, including perhaps Darcy's titled relations, I am not of much consequence, as the Bennets have never been prominent. But I will always be more acceptable than your brother, regardless of his wealth.

"I know you understand this, else you would not be nearly so desperate to catch Darcy at all costs." Bennet nodded toward the man, who danced with Bennet's daughter down the line in front of them. "Again, I have no intention of offending. It is merely the truth. Had I wished it, I may have looked down my nose at your brother as new money. But I care not for a man's situation. Character is far more important.

"Regarding Darcy," continued Bennet companionably as the woman continued to churn with anger, "an intelligent woman must perceive the truth. I am not so old that I do not remember the first stirrings of passion. If Darcy does not propose to my daughter before Christmas, the boy will surprise me very much. Unless I am no judge at all, your brother will propose to Jane before then."

"It shall not be!" hissed the woman. "I shall not allow it. Triumph shall be mine, despite whatever your improper daughters might attempt!"

With those words, Miss Bingley spun and marched away, her frame rigid with the strain of fury. Bennet watched her go, idly wondering if he ought to do something to thwart her obvious intention to have Darcy for herself, whatever his feelings on the subject.

Consider it though he did, Bennet ultimately decided against it. Bingley was ready to take his sister from Netherfield, meaning she would have little time in which to spin her webs. Moreover, Bennet had every confidence in Darcy's ability to protect himself from Miss Bingley. The Darcy he knew would never allow her to dictate his future life. Thus, Bennet settled in to watch the fun, confident his daughters' futures would be secure before long.

When the dust of that evening settled, Bennet would reflect upon how much of a mistake he had made.

"Have you noted how much time Charlotte has spent in Mr. Collins's company?"

"Yes, Mary, I have." Elizabeth smiled at her younger sister. "It is quite a strange pairing, is it not?"

"Mr. Collins would make a strange pairing with *anyone*," muttered Mary.

Elizabeth nodded to her sister in complete agreement. Grateful to her father for interceding when Mr. Collins thought to make himself agreeable to them, she had largely avoided contemplating the parson, content with the thought that he would be there a matter of two weeks and return to his parish. Elizabeth had never considered the possibility that he might find someone else on whom to bestow his attentions, and the thought that sensible Charlotte Lucas might welcome him had warranted even less consideration.

Given what Elizabeth had seen that evening, however, it was difficult to ascribe any other interpretation to Charlotte's actions. The time Mr. Collins had spent at Lucas Lodge of late further excited Elizabeth's suspicions. Mary had turned her attention to other matters, but Elizabeth continued to regard her friend; after a time of this, a resolution built within her to request an accounting from Charlotte. The opportunity to do exactly that arose a few moments later when Mr. Collins moved away from Charlotte in the direction of the refreshment table.

"Charlotte," greeted Elizabeth as she stepped close to her friend.

"Lizzy," replied Charlotte, her tone even, betraying nothing of her feelings.

Her friend's distant greeting brought Elizabeth to a halt, for she had the distinct impression her friend understood her and had expected her to approach. Elizabeth made some attempt at their usual brand of lively conversation, but she could see it did not fool Charlotte at all. It made for a few stilted moments, such a situation as she had never experienced with her friend.

"Lizzy," said Charlotte, "please allow me to address this subject which is foremost in your thoughts, so we may put it behind us. Might I assume you wonder about my apparent contentment in Mr. Collins's company?"

Dumbfounded, Elizabeth stared at her friend and then burst into laughter. "It appears you know me better than I know myself."

"It was not difficult, Lizzy. Your growing curiosity has been palpable all evening. Please let me assure you that Mr. Collins is not intruding on my good nature. I am quite content to be his companion."

Elizabeth regarded her friend for a long moment. "Never would I have thought that, Charlotte, for I know you would have no trouble dispensing with him if you wished it. Your motives for staying close to him are not so clear."

"Can you not guess, Elizabeth?"

As it happened, Elizabeth could guess very well. The notion was so odd, that she was uncertain if she should give it any credence.

"Consider my situation," continued Charlotte when Elizabeth did not speak. "I am seven and twenty and have no prospects. My understanding is that your father warned Mr. Collins away from you and your sisters; while I cannot speak for Mary and Kitty, it appears he was correct about you and Jane. *If* he is not to have one of you, may I not draw his attention to me?"

"But he is such a man," said Elizabeth.

"Are you accusing him of anything specific, Lizzy?"

There was a hard edge in Charlotte's reply, such that Elizabeth did not think she had ever heard directed to her.

"No, I know nothing of Mr. Collins to say that he is not

respectable." Elizabeth regarded her friend, determined she understood what she wished to say. "But he is also not a man I would wish for you, my dear friend. While I will not belittle the man, he possesses qualities I suspect will not make him an agreeable companion."

"I understand what you are saying, Elizabeth," said Charlotte. "And I appreciate your circumspection. At the same time, I ask for your support. Do you suppose I cannot determine for myself if a man will make an acceptable companion for *me*?"

With a sigh, Elizabeth nodded, knowing her friend was correct. There was no one of Elizabeth's acquaintance she could better trust to know her mind.

"Of course, I trust you, Charlotte."

"Then please allow me to follow my path, and do not involve yourself, Lizzy."

"Very well," said Elizabeth, throwing her arms around Charlotte. "If you should succeed, no one will more fervently express their hopes for your happiness than I."

"Thank you, Lizzy." Charlotte's voice trembled. "Your support is as important to me as Mama and Papa's."

"What excellent felicity is this!"

Stepping away from Charlotte, Elizabeth noted that Mr. Collins had returned, carrying two cups of punch. He regarded them, a beatific yet slightly silly smile on his face.

"I hope, my dear cousin, that we can count on the privilege of your association, for having just returned to the bosom of my family, I would not lose your society. The excellent friendship you possess with Miss Lucas should not be cast aside lightly."

It was an almost sensible speech if one did not consider how he alluded to his future with Charlotte, though to Elizabeth's sure knowledge, he had offered no proposal. A glance at Charlotte informed Elizabeth that her friend was determined to ignore the man's indiscretion. There was nothing else she could do but follow suit.

"Indeed, Mr. Collins, I do not think anything could convince me to give up Charlotte's friendship."

The parson beamed yet again, and Elizabeth took this opportunity to excuse herself, leaving them in each other's company. Elizabeth took herself to the side of the dance floor to consider Charlotte and her chances of happiness. While marriage to Mr. Collins would have been pure punishment for Elizabeth, after a few moments' thought, she was forced to acknowledge that Charlotte was a different woman. Several comments her friend had made over the years informed Elizabeth that Charlotte was not a romantic. That was fortunate, indeed, for Elizabeth must question the sanity of any idealist who looked on Mr. Collins with favor.

"A penny for your thoughts?"

Elizabeth looked up from her consideration into Mr. Darcy's face and smiled. "Are you certain you wish to know?"

"If it is not a subject that will scar me for life. Such as a confession you mean to accept Mr. Collins after all."

Elizabeth laughed, and Mr. Darcy joined her. "No, that is not possible now, even if I wished it. My friend, Charlotte Lucas, appears to have rendered it a hopeless business."

Mr. Darcy turned and regarded them. "I had noticed a closeness between them, but I had thought your friend too sensible."

"As had I," replied Elizabeth. "But she assures me she understands the situation and can make her own decision, and I shall wish her joy, should he proceed."

"An understandable resolve," replied Mr. Darcy. "Then, if you are not to be so fortunate as to draw the inestimable Mr. Collins to you, perhaps I would be a worthy substitute? I believe the next dance is the supper set. If you are not engaged . . . ?"

With a smile, Elizabeth nodded and allowed him to lead her to the floor.

As always, no time with Mr. Darcy could be wasted, for the gentleman was as interesting as ever. Miss Bingley did not appear to appreciate his choice for the supper sets, but Elizabeth was far from caring for the woman's opinion and ignored her, choosing instead to focus all her attention on Mr. Darcy.

Thereafter, Elizabeth allowed him to escort her into the dining room, seating herself beside him, eager to continue their conversation. The meal was excellent, as was the rest of the evening, one fault Elizabeth could not lay at Miss Bingley's door. Mr. Bingley and Jane sat next to them, and the four exchanged jests, laughing and talking together as they ate.

At length, Mr. Bingley requested a song, and his sisters obliged them on the pianoforte. Elizabeth listened critically, noting that while Miss Bingley was the technically superior musician, Mrs. Hurst's playing was more pleasing, due in part to her feeling for the music, and her lack of unnecessary accents and trills Elizabeth had always thought pretentious. For a wonder, Miss Bingley did not look to Mr.

Darcy to see if he listened to her performance with what she thought was the proper level of appreciation. She was not gracious when the company applauded, holding her head high and nodding as if it was nothing less than her due. At least she did not make a scene and attempt to draw Mr. Darcy's eyes to her.

Those following Mrs. Hurst's performance were neither so skilled nor did they play pieces so demanding as the Bingley sisters. Of these, Mary was the best, her technical prowess gained over many years of diligent practice, for Mary loved the pianoforte. Elizabeth declined to share her talents, such as they were, not having practiced anything in advance. She noted Miss Bingley's sneer in her direction, but the woman turned away and Elizabeth felt no need to respond.

After dinner, Mr. Darcy rose, informing Elizabeth that he would return shortly, leaving her sitting with Jane and Mr. Bingley. For a few moments, she sat with them, sharing a lively conversation, waiting for Mr. Darcy's return. Mr. Bingley, she knew, would direct them all back to the ballroom before long, and Elizabeth wished to spend a few more precious moments in Mr. Darcy's company.

Soon, Elizabeth wondered why the gentleman did not return. A glance around the room revealed nothing until she noted him standing on the far side near an entrance speaking with a servant. A moment later Mr. Darcy nodded, turned to look about the room, and turned to the exit, provoking a hot stab of disappointment in Elizabeth's breast. She debated the merits of following him before she determined it would not be proper.

Then she saw Miss Bingley near the same door a few minutes later. The woman glanced around, then she fairly fled through the open door through which Mr. Darcy had passed earlier. Concerned, and knowing of Miss Bingley's obsession with capturing Mr. Darcy, Elizabeth rose to her feet.

"Lizzy?" asked Jane.

"Miss Bingley; and Mr. Darcy," said she, not coherently.

Though Jane and Mr. Bingley asked her what she meant, Elizabeth could not spare the time for them. Instead, she hurried between the tables toward the door and made her way through it to the darkened hallway beyond. For an instant, Elizabeth waited for her eyes to adjust to the sudden darkness. Then a sound down the hall drew her further.

Not long after, Elizabeth came across an open door to what she knew was the library. Uncertain, and fearing what she might find, Elizabeth stepped into the room.

Just in time to see Miss Bingley make her way around a chair and fling herself into it. The chair was occupied. A tall man—Mr. Darcy—sitting therein started with shock, his arms reflexively reaching out to steady the woman who had just unceremoniously dropped herself into his lap.

"Mr. Darcy!" cried Miss Bingley dramatically. "How long I have waited for you to make this move. My dearest love, I shall accept whatever assurances you offer, for I have prayed for this day for many years!"

Shocked, Elizabeth could only watch dumbly. It did not escape her attention that the buttons on Miss Bingley's dress were undone, exposing her undergarments to the man in the chair.

Elizabeth was not dismayed. Though the woman had schemed to entrap Mr. Darcy, he had assured her that he would never bow to her maneuvers. Thus, she stepped forward, intending to give the detestable Miss Bingley a piece of her mind!

CHAPTER XI

*D*arcy was confused. While he might have thought Miss Bingley capable of engineering some stratagem to put him in a position where he would need to offer for her or suffer the consequences, if she had, the woman had emptied her quiver in vain. It appeared she had missed her mark. Darcy had intended to procure glasses of punch for himself and Miss Elizabeth, but a footman interrupted him before he could do so.

"Mr. Darcy," the man had said, "you are wanted in the small parlor in the back of the house by your valet."

Darcy had regarded the man with no little suspicion. "Did Snell tell you this himself?"

"He did, sir. He was not forthcoming about the reason for his need of you, but he was insistent that you must join him at once."

For a long moment, Darcy regarded the footman, trying to see some hint of falsehood in him. It was not beyond possibility that Miss Bingley had coached him in this matter and Darcy was not familiar enough with the Netherfield staff to know if they would put principle aside for a few coppers.

In the end, there was little enough to do but thank the man for his message and send him on his way. Darcy considered ignoring the summons, but he decided instead to spring the trap, for he did not wish to dodge Miss Bingley until he was ready to propose to Miss Elizabeth. Thus, allowing for no further consideration, he glanced about, and not seeing Miss Bingley, suspecting she was waiting for him in the parlor, he stalked from the room.

Nothing awaited him in the room the footman had indicated. While Darcy strode down the dim hall with purpose, when he neared the door, he slowed, not wishing to barge inside and have the woman throw herself into his arms and claim a compromise. When he approached the door and peered inside, it was devoid of life.

Cautiously, Darcy stepped inside, noting the furniture dotting the small chamber, the cold state of the fireplace, and the lack of any movement. It occurred to him that he would not put it past Miss Bingley to hide behind the furniture, but a quick reconnaissance of the room put such thoughts from his mind. Miss Bingley was not waiting for him.

Knowing the other possibility was for her to enter thereafter and surprise him, Darcy took a position on the other side of a sofa facing the door and waited for her to appear. In this, he was also proven incorrect, for he stood for several moments without seeing a hint of activity. Soon enough time passed that he knew the optimal time for her attempt had lapsed; even she would not be so foolish as to believe she would catch him unaware if she arrived in such a tardy fashion.

Darcy allowed a few more moments to pass before he gave the matter up as an attempt gone awry by some means he could not fathom. Thus, he took himself from the room, shaking his head at her stupidity, and made his way back to the ballroom, intent on spending a few more precious minutes in Miss Elizabeth's company. Perhaps, mused he as he walked, he could ask her to dance the last sets with him. He did not know if she would agree, for three dances at one ball would be an unmistakable show of favor. If she did not, he would understand, but her lure was so irresistible that he knew he would ask regardless of the possibility of rejection.

A movement in the hall ahead of Darcy caught his attention, coalescing into the form of a woman, who stopped at the door to the library. As Darcy watched, she stepped forward and disappeared from his sight. It was Miss Elizabeth.

Abandoning caution, Darcy rushed forward, entering the room after Miss Elizabeth in time to see her whirl and face a chair situated with its back to the door. In the chair sat a man with a woman draped over him. Behind him, he heard someone else enter, but he had no opportunity to consider that. Before Miss Elizabeth could speak, the man in the chair addressed the woman in his lap.

"Unfortunately for me, Miss Bingley, I believe you have mistaken my identity."

The sardonic tones of the man's voice revealed him to be Mr. Bennet.

Miss Bingley—for Darcy could now see it was she—stared into the man's face. Then she reacted as if his words had scalded her, scrambling from his lap, a look of horror fixed on him. When her hand went to her breast in utter shock, Darcy noted her dress hung about her shoulders, revealing her chemise beneath. Then, predictably, she became angry.

"Mr. Bennet!" exclaimed she at the same time Darcy heard Bingley's voice behind him saying: "Caroline!"

"Mr. Bennet?" another voice asked.

Darcy turned, noting that Bingley had entered the room with Miss Bennet, and behind them, a lady of the neighborhood had followed them in. Darcy did not know her, but he saw the look of avid interest in her eyes, the way she devoured the scene as if it were some tasty morsel for her to sample.

Hearing her voice, Bennet shot out of his chair. When he caught sight of her face, the color drained from his.

"Mr. Bennet!" continued the woman more forcefully. "After all these years after your excellent wife's death, now you find comfort in a woman's arms in such a manner? I have never seen such a disgusting scene as this!"

With that, the woman turned on her heel and hurried away. Silence reigned in her wake until Bennet murmured: "Well, that will put the fox among the hens."

"Why are you here, Mr. Bennet?" demanded Miss Bingley, her affront seeming to blind her to the implications of what had just happened.

"I might ask you the same, Miss Bingley," was Mr. Bennet's wry response. It appeared the man had already resigned himself to his situation. "I am acknowledged as a man who does not enjoy society. After dinner, I thought to gain a brief respite from the press and spend a few quiet moments in Mr. Bingley's sadly lacking library."

Incongruously to the situation, Bennet shot a grin at Bingley, who returned it with some ferocity. Miss Bingley, however, was not happy. Unaware of her disheveled state, she caught sight of Darcy.

"Mr. Darcy was supposed to be in that chair! It was *him* with whom

I had an assignation, not *you!*"

"That, I categorically deny," replied Darcy. "After I ate dinner with Miss Elizabeth, my valet summoned me to speak with him." Miss Bingley did not need to know he had not so much as seen Snell — her machinations would work against her. "I have only just arrived now."

Miss Bingley regarded Darcy, fear staining her countenance. It was fortunate that Bingley asserted himself at that moment.

"Let us consider this event rationally," said he, moving into the room to confront them all. "I apologize for my sister's actions, Bennet. We all know what happened here, and I do not blame you. Caroline may fix her appearance, and we should return to the ball. With any luck, we can keep this matter hushed."

Mr. Bennet chuckled, a particularly mirthless sound. "I am afraid it is not that easy, Bingley. The lady who so thoroughly castigated me is none other than Mrs. Long. She is one of the few ladies in the community who outstripped my late wife's penchant for gossip. Even now, I suspect that tales of this scandalous scene are winging their way through your guests."

A collective groan made its way through the company, though no one made a sound. Miss Bingley, it appeared, finally understood the consequences of her actions, though she set her jaw, revealing her intention to deny them. Darcy looked at the scene with something akin to chagrin, while at the same time he could not deny he felt strangely relieved. It would not be he who must put Miss Bingley off and refuse to honor a commitment he had not made. Bennet, on the other hand, might benefit from marriage to Miss Bingley, if he could refrain from strangling the woman. Darcy was uncertain he could have held himself back in similar circumstances.

In the back of Darcy's mind, however, he wondered at the apparent mistake. Darcy had been correct to suspect Miss Bingley of furthering her attempts to compromise him. Yet, she had done so with Bennet in another location from where she had intended to entrap him. Was she so little acquainted with the house that she could not even appear in the room she had thought to use?

"Let us consider this rationally," said Bingley, interrupting Darcy's consideration. "How long were you here before my sister came, Bennet?"

"Perhaps only a few moments," replied Bennet. "I had begun to doze a little when your sister appeared." Bennet directed a sidelong glance at Miss Bingley and added: "I was not aware of your undying love for me, Miss Bingley. It is difficult to fathom how I might have provoked it."

"I meant it for *him!*" exclaimed Miss Bingley, pointing one boney finger at Darcy. "I thought he was you."

Bingley's gaze passed between Darcy and Bennet, and he shook his head. "I have never noted it before, but you are similar in height, and from behind, I can understand how my sister might have mistaken your identity in the dimness."

"It matters not," spat Miss Bingley. "My assignation was with Mr. Darcy. It was he who compromised me."

"I am afraid that is not how this works, Caroline," said Bingley with a rueful shake of his head. "We all—including Mrs. Long—saw you on Bennet's knee. As Darcy was standing there and she saw both of their faces, Mrs. Long cannot have mistaken the two men."

"That is the salient point," said Bennet. "Had Mrs. Long not entered the room, I would be quite content to allow the matter to rest and forget it ever happened."

"Do you expect me to marry *you*," demanded Miss Bingley. Her disdainful gaze flayed Bennet, excoriating him where he stood. "That is nonsensical, for I shall not oblige. I was meant for greater things than to be married to a minor country gentleman."

"Miss Bingley," said Bennet, "I know not what you believe your destiny to have been. However, the mores of society are clear in this situation. If you refuse to marry me, you will not only ruin your reputation, but you will affect mine. Perhaps you may leave Meryton and never return. But I must remain. I am not in a position where gossip will not affect me. Or my daughters, for that matter.

"This is a situation of your doing. I have spoken of my willingness to restore your reputation by offering honorable marriage. I would appreciate it if you did not denigrate my name and position, given it is far greater than what you can boast."

"Of course, Caroline must cease her baseless attacks," said Bingley when his sister opened her mouth to speak.

One glare silenced her, though Darcy knew she was not cowed. Then Bingley turned to Miss Bennet and Miss Elizabeth.

"It appears I must take action. Would you find my sister, Mrs. Hurst, and send her to me? I believe it would be best if she assumed the role of mistress and Caroline retired for the night."

"Very well, Mr. Bingley," said Miss Bennet.

Miss Bingley did not appear to be pleased with her brother's instructions, but Miss Elizabeth nodded and coaxed her sister to follow her from the library. While they waited for Mrs. Hurst to arrive, Darcy stood considering the situation, while Bingley argued with his sister. Bennet appeared to be in the same straits as Darcy. A suspicion had appeared in the back of Darcy's mind, and he now wished to discover the truth.

"Charles?"

"Ah, Louisa," said Bingley when she entered the room.

He pulled her to the side with his younger sister, gesturing toward her and telling her an abbreviated account of what had occurred. Darcy wondered if Mrs. Hurst had been involved, but one look at the woman's shocked features and the harsh look she directed at her sister revealed she had not been part of Miss Bingley's schemes. A few moments later, Mrs. Hurst led her sister from the room. With any luck, Darcy would not see the woman again that evening. Then Bingley turned back to Darcy and Bennet.

"Bennet, you have my apologies for my sister's behavior."

"It is hardly your fault, Bingley," said Bennet, waving him off.

"No, it is not. Yet I feel responsible all the same."

Bennet shook his head, then he fixed Bingley with a demanding look. "Do you suppose your sister will continue to refuse me? I was not exaggerating when I said her reputation would suffer, as will mine."

"Especially if any word of this makes its way to town," said Darcy. "You have my apologies, my friend, but your sister has enough notoriety in London to completely ruin her should word of this reach the ears of the gossips."

"And we do not possess the status which would allow us to withstand what they will say of her," replied Bingley. "I know, my friend. This is a disaster."

"Had Mrs. Long not come upon us, we could have ignored this ever happened," observed Mr. Bennet. He cast a long look at Bingley. "Do you suppose she engineered Mrs. Long's presence?"

"It is impossible to say," said Bingley. "But I shall speak to her of it." Bingley turned to Darcy. "What I cannot understand is how she came to make this attempt at all."

Darcy shrugged, unwilling to speculate at the moment and unwilling to further complicate matters. "What is important is that it has happened. We must consider what we must do to ensure your sister acts in a way that will not make the situation worse."

"Caroline will do as she must," said Bingley, steel in his voice such as Darcy had never heard from him. "I will make sure of it."

Bennet nodded his head, a great weariness seeming to have settled over him. "At present, I do not wish to discuss this further. I should think tomorrow will be soon enough."

"Very well," said Bingley. "Perhaps we should meet tomorrow morning."

"That is agreeable. With your sister retired to her room, I believe it would be equally advisable that I do not appear in the company again. If you will advise my daughters, I believe we shall return to Longbourn at once."

"That would be for the best," agreed Darcy.

A moment later, Darcy departed in Bingley's company. His suspicions had been aroused in the interim, Darcy meant to confirm the truth of his conjecture. First, he must speak to Miss Elizabeth and ensure they understood each other.

It was clear the moment that Elizabeth stepped back into the dining room that Mrs. Long had already found fertile ground for her gossiping. Had the sudden cessation of sound, the way those in attendance regarded her not informed her of the truth of the matter, the sly, speculative looks she received would have spoken without the ability to misunderstand. Jane sought out Mrs. Hurst, who appeared to have heard something of the evening's events, for she rushed away the moment Jane shared a few low words with her.

"Jane," said Elizabeth, when her sister turned her attention back to her, "we should gather Kitty and Mary, for I doubt Papa will wish to remain."

While she might have protested, Jane saw the wisdom in this at once. "We should find Mr. Collins too."

Little though the thought of making Mr. Collins aware of the night's troubles pleased her, Elizabeth agreed it was for the best. Separating, they searched for their younger sisters, Elizabeth finding Kitty speaking with an officer only a few moments later.

"Come Kitty," said she, beckoning to her sister. "I have need of you at once."

"Lizzy!" hissed Kitty, though she did not protest Elizabeth's command. "Is it true? Denny told me our father was caught in flagrante delicto with Miss Bingley in the bushes outside."

Elizabeth rolled her eyes. "Do you suppose they would be outside in such a fashion given the chill of the season?"

Kitty opened her mouth to speak, but Elizabeth forestalled her. "Something *has* happened, Kitty, but it appears the story has grown with the telling. You will know what it is soon enough, but now I would ask you to hold your tongue."

The girl did not appear to appreciate Elizabeth's directive, but she did not speak. Soon, they found Mary and Jane, and they stood together by the side of the room, noting the looks they were receiving, wishing they would just go away. Soon Mr. Collins joined them, full of questions, but Elizabeth ignored him.

Salvation arrived in the form of Mr. Bingley. The gentleman arrived and called for the attention of his guests, suggesting they return to the ballroom for the rest of the evening. The gentleman could not divert the gossip so easily, but no one protested, and soon the room cleared. Mr. Darcy, who had entered with his friend, approached the Bennet sisters at once, his face a mask of concern.

"Miss Elizabeth," said he, his forced smile falling on them all. "Your father has requested your presence, for he wishes to leave at once."

"As I suspected," replied Elizabeth with a nod. "Have you decided upon anything yet?"

"It is clear what must be done," replied Mr. Darcy with a shake of his head. "The issue will be to convince my friend's sister."

"What has happened?" demanded Kitty.

"Quiet, Kitty," instructed Elizabeth. "You will learn soon enough."

The girl was not pleased, but she subsided. Mr. Darcy gave her a kindly smile, then he gestured to draw Elizabeth away from her sisters.

"Do not concern yourself, Miss Elizabeth. My friend assures me he will require his sister to acknowledge her errors and abide by the consequences."

"That is well, Mr. Darcy," said Elizabeth. "But what of my father? I cannot imagine he will be happy with Miss Bingley for a wife."

"Perhaps he will surprise you, Miss Elizabeth," replied Mr. Darcy. "Many a marriage has begun in indifference or dislike. In time, they may become resigned to their situation."

"We can only hope."

With a nod, Darcy gathered her hand and pressed a kiss to it. "Then I shall see you soon, tomorrow if I can arrange it."

"I shall anticipate it."

With a last smile, the gentleman turned and marched from the room, his stride filled with purpose. Elizabeth noted that Mr. Bingley had taken the opportunity to farewell Jane and had now moved to follow his friend. Soon thereafter, the Bennet sisters found themselves alone.

Contrary to Kitty's demands to know what had happened at once, their father would say nothing while they waited for their coach, apparently consumed with his thoughts. When the carriage arrived, he handed his daughters within, motioning to Mr. Collins to precede him into the carriage, and instructed the driver to depart, settling in as if he had never been wearier in his life. Then Kitty's patience snapped.

"Papa!" wailed she. "Will you not tell us what happened?"

"If I could, I would wish to forget tonight ever happened," rumbled Mr. Bennet. "But it is a situation that cannot be ignored, that will change our lives forever."

Then he informed his two youngest daughters what had happened, leaving nothing out. What they knew was simple enough and did not take long in the telling. The two girls appeared astonished at what they were hearing, but this surprise did not extend to locking their tongues.

"What an odious woman she is!" exclaimed Mary. "What willful disregard for the laws of God and men!"

"How is such a thing to be fathomed?" asked Kitty. "Miss Bingley for a mother? It is beyond comprehension!"

"Perhaps that is so," said Mr. Bennet. "But it appears we must grasp it, regardless of our wish it was otherwise. Even if I was inclined to ignore the event I cannot do so, for Mrs. Long will not have lost any time in disseminating what she saw to everyone in attendance."

"The gossip was already widespread by the time we returned to the dining room," said Elizabeth miserably.

Mr. Bennet chuckled, incongruous to the situation. "I must commend Mrs. Long. The speed with which she spread her tales would have impressed even your mother."

"Then have you decided on a date for a wedding?" asked Jane.

"We have not," replied Mr. Bennet. "The prospective bride is not exactly willing."

"She has no choice," said Elizabeth far more sharply than she had intended. "She provoked this mess; the responsibility to repair it must also be hers."

"Yet, Miss Bingley is not a woman to relinquish what she believes she deserves."

"And she has a right to Mr. Darcy?"

Bennet chuckled. "I share your indignation, Lizzy, though at this point there appears to be little use for it. No, I dare say she has no right to dictate to any of us, least of all to me. What I cannot quite determine is how her aim went so awry. I accept that she might have mistaken me for Darcy in the dim light of the library. But I cannot understand how she could have thought Darcy would be in that room rather than me."

"This is a most distressing incident, Cousin," Mr. Collins spoke up at last. "I might not have thought Miss Bingley so lacking in common decency. Perhaps I should suggest to Mr. Darcy that he give up the friendship, for the woman is clearly not worthy of it."

"You will do as you think you should," said Mr. Bennet. "But I would remind you that the Bingleys will likely be a close connection shortly. As Darcy has expressed an undeniable interest in Elizabeth, I doubt he can now avoid the acquaintance."

Mr. Collins peered at him, clearly unhappy with what Mr. Bennet had said. In the end, he did not speak again, surprising, considering his verbosity, though his discretion was welcome. They fell silent thereafter, even Kitty's uncertainty relieving her of any further comment. The rest of the journey to Longbourn passed in silence, each of its occupants fixed on their thoughts.

How Elizabeth felt, she could not say. The notion of her father resigning himself to what must be an objectionable situation with Miss Caroline Bingley was onerous, yet she did not know what she could do to stop it. Miss Bingley had sealed her fate and Mr. Bennet's with her grasping ways and reprehensible behavior. Surely there was no way out of the noose in which she had placed their necks.

"Papa," said Kitty in a small voice as they sighted Longbourn through the trees.

"Yes, Kitty, my dear?"

The girl struggled for a moment to say what she wished, though Elizabeth could see her beseeching eyes in the gloom of the carriage. A moment later she appeared to pluck up her courage.

"This business of you marrying Miss Bingley . . . I cannot imagine she will be an agreeable mother."

Mr. Bennet's mien softened, and he grasped his youngest daughter's hand. "Do not make yourself unhappy, Kitty. Perhaps the circumstances are not the best, but I shall not allow her to mistreat you or your sisters. After a time, I dare say she will become accustomed to her situation."

Kitty attempted a tremulous smile, and she nodded, her confidence bolstered by her father's assurances. The carriage pulled up to the front door of the house and Bennet alighted, helping his daughters from the conveyance. They entered within, handing their outerwear to the waiting Mrs. Hill, and from thence made their way further into the house.

"Let us retire at once, girls, for I have no wish to discuss this business ad nauseum. I hope it will appear less bleak by the light of the morning sun."

"I agree, Papa," said Elizabeth. "Come, sisters, let us return to our rooms."

Their father made no move, appearing content to watch them as they climbed the stairs; Elizabeth was certain he would seek the comforts of his study. Elizabeth doubted he would sleep that night — she doubted she would sleep herself. It was fortunate her father was not a man to imbibe to excess, for the thought of enduring Caroline Bingley for a lifetime must provoke a wish for oblivion, if only for a short time. It was akin to Elizabeth marrying Mr. Collins. The thought provoked a shudder to run down her spine.

CHAPTER XII

"Caroline will be the death of me!"

It was not the first time Bingley had reiterated that refrain, the repetition provoking no small measure of mirth in Darcy's breast. That Miss Bingley had not compromised *him* allowed Darcy to see the humor in it—had she achieved her design, Darcy imagined he would be in a far worse state than Bingley. Given what he had learned the previous evening, Darcy knew it had not been providence, but a direct hand that had ensured his survival.

Darcy did not wish to think about that. It would be better if it never saw the light of day, that he did not consider it again, even for an instant. As such, he pushed such thoughts away and concentrated on his friend. Bingley was not a man to pace, not in the entire time Darcy had known him. Yet that morning he appeared as if he were about to wear a hole in the carpet.

"My own sister, engaged in such disgusting behavior!" exclaimed Bingley. "How can I even comprehend such conduct as this?"

"Then she confessed to plotting last night's excitement?"

Bingley shot Darcy a hard look; Darcy felt an urgent need to stifle a chortle, for he knew Bingley's look was not in censure of him. "In fact, I could induce her to confess nothing. She kept claiming that she was *not* compromised and that the notion she must marry Bennet was laughable. In between the lines, however, I have learned enough to know what she did, though I am completely at sea about how it all went awry. The footman insists that your man informed him of your desire to meet him in the parlor and will not recant. I cannot determine the truth."

"It is unfortunate, but unless the principals in the affair confess, it is doubtful you will ever know what happened."

With a disgusted huff, Bingley agreed and resumed his pacing. "The worst is that I feel that I have betrayed a man of whom I think highly."

"It is not your fault, Bingley," reminded Darcy. "Your sister is a woman full grown, one aware of the consequences of her actions. You cannot blame yourself for her missteps."

"I know, Darcy. But that does not make the situation easier to bear."

Darcy watched his friend for a long moment. It *was* true, he supposed, that part of the reason his sister had become the way she had was that Bingley was a man who did not like conflict and had tolerated her behavior for years. The problem, Darcy suspected, was much older than Bingley's stewardship over his family's affairs, for Darcy was certain her parents had indulged Miss Bingley as the youngest. A little firmness on Bingley's part might have blunted the worst of her excesses, but Darcy knew full well his friend had not possessed the influence to change her.

"From a certain point of view," said Darcy, "your sister will receive exactly what she deserves."

Bingley snorted. "You only say that because you will not bear the consequences of her folly."

"I own it without disguise," replied Darcy, receiving his friend's feral grin for his trouble. "I am heartily grateful that your sister's aim went awry, though I will note that I would not have capitulated, regardless."

"As you have avowed before." Bingley sighed heavily and threw himself into a chair, resting his chin in one hand and brooding. "The worst of this business is that I think highly of Bennet. While you say that Caroline will reap what she has sown, Bennet is blameless in this matter. Yet he must also bear the consequences."

"The way you speak," said Darcy, restraining his laughter, "it appears you do not consider your sister an excellent catch."

Bingley felt no such self-control, barking a laugh. "I cannot say what sort of man deserves Caroline, but I do not think Bennet deserves her. She will make his life miserable."

"Perhaps she will; or perhaps Bennet is made of sterner stuff than you believe. Consider this, Bingley: marrying your sister might work to Bennet's advantage."

"How so?" asked Bingley, confused by Darcy's assertion.

"The entail," clarified Darcy. "Bennet has provided for his daughters, but any man wishes to pass his legacy off to his offspring. Your sister is young and healthy, allowing Bennet to hope for a son, a prospect he has not had in many years."

The observation drew Bingley's brooding to a halt, rendering him contemplative for the first time that morning. "I had not considered it in such a way."

"No, I did not suppose you had. It would not surprise me if Bennet has not considered it either. As I am not directly connected with this affair, I am not so ruled by emotion, rendering me much better able to consider less immediate consequences."

Bingley nodded slowly. "Yes, I can see that, my friend. But you forget one thing."

"Which is?" asked Darcy.

"The condition of our friend's sanity once he has Caroline for a wife. I would not doubt she will drive him to Bedlam within a week!"

Darcy could not help but laugh with his friend, for his observation was all too apropos. Were Darcy in Bennet's position, he would have doubted his ability to cling to his sanity, for he could not imagine living with Caroline Bingley would be at all conducive to a happy life. It was possible, however, that Bennet could even thrive in the circumstances in which he found himself.

"Consider the practicalities of the situation," said Darcy, drawing his friend's attention again. "If she married me, she would think she had the means at her disposal to do whatever she wished. With my position in society, we would always bicker over our attendance, how long we would remain in London, and what events we would attend. With Bennet, however, much of that will not be an issue."

Again, Bingley became contemplative. "Because Bennet is a more modest country gentleman and does not have a presence in town."

"Exactly," replied Darcy. "They will disagree—no married couple can avoid occasional disagreements. But Miss Bingley will need to be content with Meryton and society here, and she will need to learn to accept that."

"Unless she applies to you or me to host them in town."

Darcy laughed. "Do you suppose Bennet will endure it?"

"No, I suppose you are correct," said Bingley. "Though I suspect she will prevail upon occasion."

"Then leave that problem to Bennet. There is another benefit you have not considered—Miss Bingley, because of her dowry and Bennet's prominence in the neighborhood, will become one of the leading lights of local society. In time, she may even appreciate her position here, as opposed to her relatively lower standing in London."

"That is possible," conceded Bingley. "I can only hope it is so, for I foresee an unhappy marriage otherwise."

"Trust in Bennet to control his wife, Bingley," said Darcy. "When they marry, you will not be responsible for her any longer."

Bingley perked up at that observation. "That is perhaps the best part of this business, Darcy. For me, anyway. I have longed to pass her care off to someone—anyone—so that I may free myself from her conceit."

"Then stop blaming yourself and accept what you cannot change. Bennet will be well—and there are benefits for him too. In time, I suspect they will be content, if not deliriously happy."

With a nod, Bingley allowed the subject to rest. All that remained was to plan the event and ensure Miss Bingley did not refuse to do as she must. With Bingley in his present mood, Darcy suspected his sister would have no choice, but it would be best to ensure there were no misunderstandings.

Darcy felt liberated for the first time in many months. Caroline Bingley had long been a source of aggravation. Now, he no longer needed to consider how he might fend her off.

"You wish to accompany me to Netherfield?"

Elizabeth directed a glare at her father, noting his incomprehension. "I do. Miss Bingley has behaved abominably; I wish to make my sentiments known to her."

"No one could do it so well as you, Lizzy," quipped Mr. Bennet.

It was, Elizabeth knew, a capitulation, not that she had ever expected her father to forbid her from going. Miss Bingley, they all knew, would not be accepting of her situation, and all the help they could get in forcing her to the path she must take would be welcome.

"Has Collins departed?" asked Bennet.

Elizabeth could not help her glance skyward, for the parson had frayed the patience of them all that morning. From the moment he had appeared, he had persisted in denouncing what he saw as their poor behavior. Miss Bingley was an odious woman—a notion with which

Elizabeth agreed—Mr. Bennet was foolish for not foiling her bid to compromise him, the Bennet sisters were improper, and the neighborhood was, in short, deficient in every respect. Elizabeth had considered the relative merits of insulting him so much he would grow offended and leave.

"Finally," said she, her look of distaste amusing her father. "And not without a few choice words for us in parting. He is gone to Lucas Lodge, and I hope he stays there all day. If Charlotte accepts him, I must question her judgment. If he remains until Saturday as he threatened, I might go to Gracechurch Street to retain my sanity."

"He is a peculiar mix to be certain," laughed her father.

"And this after he informed Jane and me so faithfully that he would step into the breach should Mr. Darcy or Mr. Bingley falter."

Not having heard this, her father looked at her with some interest. "When did this happen?"

"The day after you warned him away from us."

"Well," chortled her father, "at least you need not worry about being forced to make a prudent decision should your beau steal away in the dead of night."

Elizabeth shook her head, unwilling to respond to the jest. Given the way Mr. Darcy had behaved the previous evening, Elizabeth suspected her future was secure. But she did not wish to discuss it at present, for there were other considerations that took precedence.

"What I cannot understand," said her father, "is how Collins has failed to understand that my remarrying puts his position as heir to this estate in jeopardy."

"Nor can I," said Elizabeth. "It would seem to me that a man in his situation would know any such threats to his future inheritance."

"Not every man is my cousin."

"Thank God for that!"

None of Elizabeth's sisters had any interest in returning to Netherfield that morning, a fact for which Elizabeth felt no small measure of gratitude. Among them, she was the only one equipped for the struggle she knew the morning's activities would present. Mr. Collins departing for Lucas Lodge that morning had been necessary, for he could not stay in the house with Mr. Bennet absent. Elizabeth knew her father had allowed certain matters on the estate to lapse because he could not leave his daughters alone with the parson. With any luck, Elizabeth hoped Mr. Collins would depart before his time, for she did not wish to endure him for another four days.

At length, Elizabeth entered the carriage with her father for the quick journey to the neighboring estate. Mr. Bingley and Mr. Darcy greeted them upon their arrival, Mr. Darcy welcoming Elizabeth with his typical warmth while Mr. Bingley looked at her in confusion, no doubt wondering why she had come. Elizabeth ignored him, and he did not press the matter; soon, he led them to the sitting-room where they were to deal with the events of the previous evening.

"Thank you for coming, Mr. Bennet," said Bingley. "Please accept my apologies again for my sister's abominable conduct last night. I can scarcely think about it without revulsion, and I know the consequences will not be agreeable."

Mr. Bennet looked at his neighbor, a hint of a smile lifting the corners of his lips. "If I read you correctly, Bingley, it appears you are speaking ill of your sister. Do you think so poorly of her?"

"Do *you* not think poorly of her?"

With a laugh, Bennet shook his head. "While I can agree her actions were deplorable, there is no reason to belabor the point. Consider this, Bingley: a man is better positioned to influence his wife to better behavior than a brother only a year or two her elder."

"Then you mean to restore your reputation by marrying her."

"There appears to be little enough choice in the matter, Darcy," said Mr. Bennet. "I knew when I departed last evening how it would end."

"If we can convince my sister," replied Mr. Bingley, a sour note in his voice.

"Aye, therein lies the rub." Mr. Bennet lost his joviality and peered at Mr. Bingley. "Do you suppose your sister will refuse?"

"I shall ensure she accepts," said Bingley, determination evident in every hint of his manner. "Caroline provoked these events. She must repair the damage she has wrought."

"I do not disagree," said Bennet. "On some level, however, I believe I would prefer a wife who is resigned at the very least. Forcing her to the altar and requiring she speak the words are a recipe for a long life of misery. If she refuses me, does she have any recourse?"

"Her own fortune," replied Mr. Bingley. "I control it now, but if she insisted, I would release it to her and set her up in a situation of her own. It would need to be in the north, for it is not enough to see her in comfort in London, but she would be independent."

"Your sister would never agree to such a thing," said Mr. Darcy. "I suspect that even a marriage she does not want would be preferable to being banished to the north with little hope of finding *any* man willing to marry her."

"Then that may be our last alternative," said her father. "It will not prompt her enthusiasm, but that I do not require. Only her submission is necessary."

"It appears it is time I summon her," said Mr. Bingley.

The man rose and called for the housekeeper, instructing her to bid Miss Bingley join them at once. Elizabeth wondered if she would deign to show her face without her brother marching her every step of the way. In this, it appeared she had misunderstood matters at Netherfield, for it was not five minutes before Miss Bingley entered the room, trailed closely by the Hursts. Given the look Mr. Hurst gave her, he appeared a jailor escorting a prisoner to a cell, and Mrs. Hurst's demeanor was little different from her husband's.

Miss Bingley said not a word. She crossed to the chair her brother motioned her to take, but she did not even do them the honor of looking at anyone, for she fixed her gaze on a point directly in front of her and would not alter. When his brother and sister had taken their chairs, Mr. Bingley addressed them all.

"Thank you for your attendance. After last night's events, we must determine what to do."

Even then Miss Bingley did not deign to speak. "Aye, that we must," said Mr. Hurst, regarding his sister out of the corner of his eye. "Perhaps you will have better luck talking some sense into her, for Louisa and I have exhausted our patience."

Mr. Bingley opened his mouth to speak to his sister, but he noted how Mr. Bennet waved him to silence and desisted. Thus far, Miss Bingley had given no indication she could even hear them, though Elizabeth thought she detected an ephemeral glance when he moved. But she did not acknowledge him, leaving Mr. Bennet to make his case.

"It appears we find ourselves in a spot of trouble, Miss Bingley. I shall not bore us all with a recitation of what has happened or recount past grievances. Instead, it appears best that we speak of the practicalities of the matter."

"You may as well save your breath, Mr. Bennet," said Miss Bingley, speaking with unexpected calmness. "Though I mean no slight, you are not the sort of gentleman I would ever marry."

"No, I do not suppose I am your first or even your hundredth choice." Mr. Bennet gave her a sardonic grin, which was wasted as she still refused to look at him. "That does not change the reality of the situation. For the restoration of both our reputations and that of our families, there is no choice but for us to marry."

"I do not acknowledge that." The laugh that issued from the woman's breast was overflowing with contempt. "Do you suppose I care two figs for what the people in this miserable neighborhood are saying? They are nothing to me."

"Do you suppose the gossip will stay confined to Meryton, Caroline?" asked Mr. Bingley, unable to hold his countenance any longer.

Miss Bingley's reply was a sneer. "No one here is of any consequence. I cannot imagine them possessing a connection to anyone in a position to attend even the meanest event in London."

"Upon my word!" exclaimed Elizabeth, disgusted with her again. "You *do* have a high opinion of yourself!"

Miss Bingley bared her teeth. "I would not expect a witless worm such as *you* to understand."

"I understand well enough," snapped Elizabeth. "Before me, I see a woman who greatly overestimates her value, who disdains those who every sane member of society would consider above her. It may have escaped your notice, Miss Bingley, but you are not a princess."

"And what are you?" spat Miss Bingley.

"The daughter of a country gentleman," rejoined Elizabeth, not giving an inch. "The difference between us is that I am not ashamed of my origins, nor do I attempt to lord my supposed superiority over everyone I meet."

Miss Bingley's jaw worked in her anger, but she did not open her mouth to respond. The woman must know she was friendless in this company, for her brother and sister looked upon her with exasperation even more than what those not related to her displayed. Mr. Bennet, Elizabeth noticed, watched her with mirth, his eyes seeming to tell her to continue speaking, inform Miss Bingley of her littleness and disgrace.

"The facts of the situation, Miss Bingley," continued Elizabeth when the other woman did not respond, "are incontrovertible. The current difficulties are of *your* creation, your offenses perpetrated in pursuit of your obsession with connecting yourself to a man who does not wish to have you. You have acted in contravention of all decency, determined to promote your desires at the expense of others.

"My father has consented to marry you, despite these deficiencies of character, decorum, and the sure expectation of a future devoid of any happiness with you as a wife. And yet, you act as if *you* are the injured party, raining injustice and scorn upon those whose forgiveness you should be begging. Are these the actions of a woman of any dignity?

"I have intimate knowledge of my father's reluctance to marry you, yet he will act as a gentleman ought and restore your reputation. Will you, a woman who pretends to high society, act in a manner befitting a gentlewoman?"

Elizabeth was not proud of her diatribe, for she had no wish to become a soulless virago like the woman before her. At the same time, she would not stand aside as this vicious shrew disdained her father, a man deserving of respect.

"That was rather harsh, Lizzy," said Mr. Bennet after a moment of silence.

"But not untrue," disagreed Mr. Bingley, his gaze fixed on his sister.

While Miss Bingley still gazed forward, refusing to look at any of them, Elizabeth could see a certain slump in her shoulders, the way she stared with misery rather than anger. Perhaps the harshness of her judgment had been necessary to remind Miss Bingley who was at fault. Elizabeth did not feel good about delivering it, but she could not repine her words, for they had been necessary.

"I appreciate your candor and your restraint," said Mr. Bingley with a nod at Elizabeth. "Given the event, I can imagine your dismay with my sister's behavior. Yet, she *is* my sister, and I would not throw her off, regardless of what she has done."

Turning back to his sister, Mr. Bingley said: "There is little choice in this matter, Caroline. A marriage to Mr. Bennet will rehabilitate your reputation, though your behavior will not win you many friends."

Miss Bingley winced, but her brother did not stop. "What it will do for you, however, is make you the wife of a gentleman. Though you may protest that Mr. Bennet's position is not what you might have wanted, it will raise our consequence in society. Is that not something to applaud?"

It would have been impossible to credit only moments before, but Miss Bingley wilted in the face of the truth. "I . . . I had always thought I would marry into the first circles." The accompanying glance she directed at Mr. Darcy was a surprise to no one.

"I informed you that I do not wish to have you as a wife, Miss Bingley." Directed at him as it was, the event might have provoked Mr. Darcy's implacable anger. Instead, his words and tone were not unkind. "I apologize, but I have never been interested in you in that way. You would do well to accept Mr. Bennet's offer, for your life will not be easy if you do not."

"Indeed," said Mr. Bingley. "The choice is yours, Sister. But I urge you not to underestimate the damage this event will do to your reputation should you choose to spurn Mr. Bennet's offer. At the very least, I cannot keep you in my household where you may ruin me at any moment."

Miss Bingley turned her displeased gaze on her brother. "You would betray me?"

"Take care about what you call betrayal," said Mr. Bingley, a stern glare for his sister. "Society could as easily perceive a betrayal as the actions of a woman who would not make amends for her mistakes."

For a long moment, Miss Bingley regarded her brother, perhaps trying to discern the extent of his resolve. What she saw was not at all to her liking, for her defiance lasted only a moment longer.

"Thank you for your *offer*, Mr. Bennet," said she, turning to look at Elizabeth's father. "I accept."

"Very well," said Mr. Bennet with a nod. "It is for the best, Miss Bingley, though I understand it does not seem so now."

While the woman returned his gesture, she did not speak again. Mr. Bingley, to Elizabeth's eyes, almost wilted with relief, and his sister and brother were in similar straits.

"I suppose we should not delay," said he to Mr. Bennet.

"There is no reason to do so and every reason to make haste," replied Mr. Bennet. "I shall apply to the parson, but I cannot see any reason he would deny us."

"Perhaps you should purchase a common license," suggested Mr. Darcy. "That way you will not need to wait for three weeks."

"Yes, that would be best," replied Bennet. He turned to Miss Bingley and gave her a hint of a smile. "I suppose I must go to London to obtain one."

The imperious nod with which Miss Bingley responded did not fill Elizabeth with hope for her father's future. It was better than the alternative.

CHAPTER XIII

One welcome consequence of the accord reached at Netherfield the morning after the ball was the departure of Mr. Collins. The parson, though he now apparently disdained his only living family, was not happy to learn that Mr. Bennet was to go to London, and even less pleased when they informed him that he could no longer stay at Longbourn as a result.

"I shall apply to Sir William to allow you to stay at Lucas Lodge for your few remaining days here," offered Mr. Bennet.

Had it been Elizabeth's decision, the situation might have tempted her to remove his effects from the house and instruct him to return to Kent. The hesitation with which he greeted Mr. Bennet's suggestion struck Elizabeth as strange, but he did not protest.

"Very well. Perhaps that is for the best, for I would not wish to damage my standing with Lady Catherine by remaining in a place so sunk in impropriety."

Mr. Bennet directed a faint smile at the parson and nodded. "A piece of advice, Cousin. When you arrive back at Rosings, I have no doubt you will speak to your patroness of what has occurred here. Take close heed of her response. I suspect it will surprise you."

The parson sniffed, but he did not reply, to the relief of them all.

Within an hour, Mr. Bennet made the application and Sir William agreed, and the Bennets were treated to the sight of Mr. Collins leaving Longbourn. Elizabeth hoped he would not return.

The very next day, Mr. Bennet left for town in the company of Mr. Bingley and Mr. Darcy, the latter having offered to allow him to stay at his house. Though the Bennets had always stayed with the Gardiners, her father accepted, knowing it would be more conveniently situated to see to his business. Mr. Darcy, Elizabeth knew, would have preferred to stay in Hertfordshire. Even with Miss Bingley's engagement, it was clear he did not wish to chance a stay in the same house without his friend present. The only time Elizabeth saw Miss Bingley, she thought the woman understood this point, though Elizabeth could not guess as to how she viewed it.

That one visit to Netherfield was the only time the Bennet sisters saw Miss Bingley those four days of their father's absence, for it became clear they were not welcome. Mrs. Hurst assured them she would handle the arrangements for her sister's wedding and breakfast, rendering the Bennets' distance acceptable. Elizabeth decided it was for the best. Netherfield would be the venue for the wedding breakfast, and Mrs. Hurst would host it, and Elizabeth had no doubt Miss Bingley would use as much of her brother's money as time permitted ensuring that in this, at least, she received all the importance she felt she deserved.

Before two days had passed, the Bennets received the surprising information that Mr. Collins had departed for Kent, a curious change of events, given what she knew of his attentions to Charlotte. The very next day, Charlotte arrived at Longbourn for a morning visit and vouchsafed the reason for his going to her dearest friend.

"Mr. Collins has already proposed?" demanded Elizabeth.

"He has," was Charlotte's simple reply.

"That is precipitous," said Elizabeth without thinking.

Charlotte, though she might have harbored some offense, smiled at Elizabeth's observation. "Yes, I suppose you might consider it impulsive. But you must understand the reality of the situation, Lizzy. Mr. Collins is a parson and cannot often leave his flock and travel to make love to me. Thus, in his mind, he must secure his future at once, especially given his falling out with your family."

"I suppose he spoke of that at length," said Elizabeth, trying to marshal her thoughts.

"I shall not sport with your intelligence by denying it," laughed Charlotte. "It appears you have taken your cousin's measure, Lizzy."

Elizabeth smiled and turned back to the subject at hand. "You have not told me of your response. Might I assume you accepted Mr. Collins's proposal?"

"I have," replied Charlotte.

"Though I would never dream of questioning your judgment," said Elizabeth carefully, "would it not have been prudent to defer that decision, or request a courtship instead?"

As Elizabeth had carefully avoided any hint of disapproval for her friend's choice, Charlotte accepted her question in the manner she had intended it. "Perhaps I might have; from my perspective, there is also a reason for haste. I am not getting any younger, Lizzy, and I judged it best to ensure my engagement to Mr. Collins was official. A man such as your cousin might forget promises to return and pay court to me in favor of whatever young woman caught his fancy in Kent."

While Elizabeth had never considered the possibility of Mr. Collins's inconstancy, she acknowledged her friend was correct. Mr. Collins struck her as a man who focused on what was before him unless it was Lady Catherine de Bourgh—in her case, he was capable of venerating her to the skies no matter the distance between them!

"Let me also say, Lizzy," continued Charlotte, "that I am not the romantic you are. I wish to have a situation of my own. As Mr. Collins is respectable and independent, I believe I shall do as well in the marriage state as any, and better than I would have had I remained at Lucas Lodge as a poor spinster sister to my brother when he comes into his inheritance."

It was a mistake Elizabeth knew she would not have—*could* not have—made had she been in Charlotte's position. It *was* Charlotte's choice, however, and she would not end their friendship by clinging to her notions of happiness in life. As such, she informed Charlotte of her support and embraced her, hoping they would somehow find a way to remain in contact with each other regardless of the parson's disgust for everything Bennet.

"In that, you may be surprised," replied Charlotte, giving her a mysterious grin. "A wife may influence a husband for the best, you know. Though Mr. Collins disapproves at present, I believe I can bring him around to the correct judgment.

"There is one other thing you should know."

"Oh? What is that?"

"Mr. Collins has not yet apprehended that your father's upcoming nuptials threaten his position as heir to this estate."

Elizabeth could not help shaking her head at the parson's apparent obtuseness. "I cannot imagine how it has escaped his comprehension."

"I shall not attempt to understand it," replied Charlotte. "At present, I have no intention of informing him of the matter, for I deem there is little point. If Miss Bingley does not produce a son, your father's marriage will not signify. If she does, he will learn when news of the event arrives in Kent. I only wished you to understand that I have accepted Mr. Collins knowing that I may never be mistress of this estate."

"Do you suppose you will be happy as a parson's wife?" asked Elizabeth with a sly grin.

Charlotte laughed at the sight. "It will not be an unfulfilling life."

"And you will have the excellent condescension and advice of the preeminent lady in all the land!"

The friends fell against each other, releasing their mirth. "In fact," continued Elizabeth, "that lady is so wise that you may leave the management of your house to her, for she will do it so much better than you!"

Charlotte sobered, the rueful shake of her head informing Elizabeth that the potential problem of her future husband's patroness had not escaped her attention. "I believe I may prevail in that regard, Lizzy. Through careful questioning, I have learned that Lady Catherine does not direct Mr. Collins nearly so much as he believes. Part of the reason her ladyship directed him to find a wife, in my opinion, is so that she can cede her direction of his activities."

"Then I wish you the best of luck, Charlotte," replied Elizabeth warmly. "I only hope we can retain our friendship."

While Charlotte did not reply, her secret smile suggested she knew something Elizabeth did not. Elizabeth decided against applying to her, for it appeared her friend wished to keep the matter to herself for the moment. If Charlotte managed her husband in Lady Catherine's stead, Elizabeth could not imagine she could not alter his opinion in the matter of the Bennets' culpability too.

As an addendum to the subject of Mr. Collins, Elizabeth found her father in his study a few days after his return, chortling over several pieces of paper he held in his hand. When Elizabeth asked him about it, he was not hesitant about explaining the reason for his mirth.

"It is a letter from Mr. Collins, Lizzy."

"Mr. Collins?" asked Elizabeth with a frown. "Did he not pledge to sever all contact with us?"

"He did, but it appears he had a change of heart." Mr. Bennet was laughing so hard that tears gathered in the corners of his eyes. "When he returned to Kent and informed his patroness of what has occurred, she responded in a manner he did not expect."

"But you did," observed Elizabeth, remembering the conversation.

"Even so self-absorbed a woman as I expect his patroness is could not fail to understand we were blameless in the matter. It appears she instructed him on the subject of forgiveness and avoiding blame, directing him to the Bible for his edification. This," Bennet held up the letter, "is six sheets of paper containing his florid apologies and groveling requests that I forgive him for it and keep up the connection."

"Given the example Lady Catherine has set for us," said Elizabeth piously, "I cannot imagine you would refuse."

"No, I will not," chortled her father, "though it is not because of Lady Catherine's instructions. My cousin's correspondence is of such color and verve that I would not forsake it for any price."

In other words, her father wished to continue to laugh at Mr. Collins's absurdities. It was quintessentially her father to desire communication for amusement. Elizabeth said nothing further, and her father returned to his contemplation of his cousin's silliness.

With the return of the gentlemen, Mr. Darcy brought his sister to Hertfordshire as promised. Miss Georgiana Darcy was a tall girl, willowy and blonde, her eyes ice blue like her brother's, her movements graceful, and her figure womanly. What she was not was confident, as Elizabeth could see at once, for she accepted their greetings with monosyllables and rarely raised her eyes from the floor.

Such a circumstance could not stand, Elizabeth determined at once, and she set to making the girl feel at ease within moments of making her acquaintance. In this both Mary and Kitty ably assisted, the former because she learned quickly that she and Miss Darcy shared a love of music, and the latter because they were of age and Kitty, eagerly, wanted her for a friend.

"I am unable to account for the changes in my sister," said Mr. Darcy to Elizabeth only a few days after his sister's coming. "This laughing creature is completely beyond my experience. It will astonish Fitzwilliam when next he sees her."

"That is your cousin, is it not?" asked Elizabeth, having heard some mention of the man.

"He is my uncle's second son," replied Mr. Darcy. "He is joined with me in Georgiana's guardianship."

Elizabeth nodded, though distracted. While Georgiana was appearing much more at ease than she had appeared when she came, she was still quieter than even Mary, though Kitty's exuberance was drawing her from her shell. Of greater concern than this in Elizabeth's eyes, was how Miss Bingley behaved. Mr. Darcy had informed Elizabeth of Miss Bingley's eager attentions to Miss Darcy, hoping to provoke Mr. Darcy's approval and proposal. She did not seem to greet Miss Darcy's affinity for Kitty's company with any grace. Elizabeth suspected this was from force of habit.

It spoke to a greater issue in her mind. Elizabeth did not think living in a house presided over by Miss Bingley would be agreeable, perhaps for her more than any of her sisters, given Mr. Darcy's focus on her. But what she could do about it, Elizabeth could not say. She could not impose upon the Gardiners for her support and staying with Uncle and Aunt Phillips was equally unpalatable. She supposed there was no choice but to endure it and hope her father acted to prevent Miss Bingley's overt misbehavior.

"Shall we not walk together behind the house, Miss Elizabeth?"

The woman turned to Darcy and smiled, indicating her consent, and they moved to the vestibule to gather their outerwear. Darcy had a particular motive for suggesting their walk, but it was also in part spurred by the quietude that had come over her. The way she observed Miss Bingley—and the way the woman's attention appeared to be fixed on them—gave Darcy some inkling of her thoughts. Miss Elizabeth's happiness had become a matter of utmost importance to Darcy, rendering the need to understand her thoughts a pressing concern.

They attained the back lawn and meandered for a time, speaking together but saying nothing of consequence. To Darcy's perception, Miss Elizabeth appeared to persist in her distraction, for all she responded to everything he said, her observations not affected by whatever was lurking in the back of her mind. In time, he acted to bring her concerns to the forefront.

"It has been a winding road to arrive at this point," said he in response to some slight comment she made on the subject, "but soon it will be over."

"When my father and his new bride will depart on their wedding tour." Miss Elizabeth paused and chuckled. "He is grateful for your offer of the house in Ramsgate for their use, but I do not think his new wife is equally eager."

"No, I suspect she is not," replied Darcy. "I will say, however, that Miss Bingley appears more resigned to her situation than I might have expected. They will come to an accord, Miss Elizabeth. Of that, I believe you need not worry."

"I have confidence in my father," said she. "It is his new wife that concerns me."

Darcy regarded her, knowing this was the crux of her disquiet. "You will be well in your father's absence?"

Miss Elizabeth turned a smile on him. "Jane is of age, and as my father has often observed, we live in a part of England so quiet as to be near insensate. We shall be quite well."

"That is unfortunate, indeed, Miss Elizabeth," replied Darcy, "for an occasional invasion of highwaymen or brigands adds a certain zest to life."

The chuckle with which she responded was half-hearted at best. Sensing she needed to disclose her feelings to him of her own accord, Darcy kept his silence in the hope she would open up to him.

"Do you truly suppose my father will be happy?"

Darcy considered the question. "There are several reasons to suppose that he will not be unhappy, Miss Elizabeth. He has another chance to father a son, which is not an inconsequential matter, as I am certain you will agree. Beyond that obvious benefit, your father strikes me as a man for whom contentment comes easily."

"Yes, I suppose he is," said Elizabeth. "Should he have his amusements and his study, I cannot imagine he will be unhappy."

Darcy nodded. "From the comments he has made about your late mother, I expect he was not precisely happy in marriage to her."

"Though I cannot remember, I suspect you are correct. My mother was no more a gentlewoman than Miss Bingley, but she was perhaps even more poorly suited to him, not having had the benefit of instruction on how to comport herself. In that, at least, she is not deficient."

"Then trust in your father to see to his satisfaction in life."

Miss Elizabeth nodded and fell silent. There was something else to her introspection—of that, Darcy was certain. It was far more likely that she would confide in him if he allowed her to do so in her own way than by pressing her. As such, Darcy waited until she spoke again.

"I am not anticipating a life at Longbourn where Miss Bingley is the mistress."

It was the perfect opening, necessitating a firm grip on himself to withhold a grin from his face. "Oh? Do you suppose she will be unkind?"

"Do you suppose she is disposed to happiness with me, in

particular?"

"No," conceded Darcy. "My knowledge of her character informs me that she considers you the means of stealing away that which she considered hers by right."

"Thus, you see my dilemma."

"Yet, I cannot imagine your father allowing her to treat you all with anything other than respect," said Darcy. "Should she attempt it, she will no doubt provoke your father's displeasure."

Miss Elizabeth nodded and sighed. "This I know. But it will remain uncomfortable for as long as I live at Longbourn."

"Why, Miss Elizabeth," said Darcy, his light tone drawing her eyes to his face, "then there is a simple solution to your problem." When Miss Elizabeth's eyebrow quirked, a demand he explain himself, Darcy was eager to explain. "If you would avoid a life with Miss Bingley, then you must depart from Longbourn. One of the best ways to do that would be to marry."

Her look at him was steady, a hint of her ever-present playful manners hiding in her smile. "Do you suppose I may accomplish that with ease? Who do you propose to put forward as my future husband?"

Darcy laughed, feeling freer than he had in many years. "It is a solemn obligation, but I believe you might persuade me to take it on myself."

"Obligation? Solemn? You *do* realize to whom you are speaking, do you not?"

"I do. In marrying you, I imagine I can expect years of bliss, Miss Elizabeth. It *is* a *solemn* duty to take on, an *obligation* I would trust to no one else."

"Smooth, Mr. Darcy," said Miss Elizabeth, her eyes alighting on him in appreciation. "You are far smoother than I might have thought when I first made your acquaintance."

"I am full of surprises, Miss Elizabeth. What say you? Shall you make me the happiest of men and accept my proposal?"

"That is something Mr. Collins might have said," replied she, her shoulders shaking so hard she could barely speak. "But it is all a moot point, for I have received no proposal, and cannot respond in the face of such a glaring deficiency."

"Then allow me to do so," said Darcy, turning to face her directly.

Miss Elizabeth, he noted, regarded him with a crooked smile, her eyes alight with anticipation. Darcy was scarcely less eager himself, for he had long known he wished to have her as a wife.

"Miss Elizabeth Bennet, I find myself enamored with your impertinence, besotted with your person, and eager to bind my life to yours forever. Will you do me the great honor of accepting my hand in marriage?"

"That is better, Mr. Darcy. I accept, of course."

The heady feeling of requited love swept over Darcy, and he leaned in, brushing her lips in their first kiss. Then he rested his forehead against hers, his arms loosely around her form as he sighed, grateful he had found his heart's desire in this, the unlikeliest of places.

At length, the air turned chill, and they moved to the house, eager to reach its confines. "I have important business with Mr. Bennet," said Darcy, prompting her brilliant smile. "I would not delay it more than an instant!"

They turned the corner of the house and approached the entrance when Bingley and Miss Bennet approached from the opposite direction. Bingley caught sight of them, and in true Bingley fashion, he approached, his hand held out for Darcy, his face etched with a wide grin.

"I say, Darcy, this is a most propitious day, for I have attained my heart's desire!"

"As have I, my friend!" laughed Darcy, provoking his friend's grip to tighten.

Miss Bennet and Miss Elizabeth, he noted came together in excited congratulations amid tears and wishes of joy. Darcy noted this, thinking that the sisters might be happier if they were situated near each other after they were married. Perhaps it might be best to advise Bingley as to the benefits of purchasing an estate closer to Pemberley.

"We must apply to Mr. Bennet at once! I shall even show you my magnanimous nature and allow you to speak to him first!"

Darcy laughed at his friend's offer. "Thank you, Bingley; I shall not spurn your gracious offer."

Together, they made their way into the house and their destinies.

After Mr. Bennet's blessings were requested and given, the two happy couples entered the sitting-room to inform the company of the day's events. Miss Georgiana Darcy squealed in delight, informing her future sister of her eagerness to have *four* new sisters, and the rest of the Bennets were scarcely less pleased. A quick look at Mr. Darcy and Charles revealed their elation, one rarely seen in the sober Mr. Darcy.

The one member of the company who did not join in the general approbation was no surprise to anyone who knew her. Louisa Hurst, who was better acquainted with her sister than any other, watched Caroline, noting her pinched expression, the way she regarded Miss Elizabeth, and — to a lesser extent — Miss Bennet with asperity. It was not a matter of *if* Caroline would say something to anger them all, but *when* she would lose control of herself and insert her foot into her mouth. Louisa determined to speak to her and prevent it.

"Look at them!" snapped Caroline when Louisa approached, though she retained enough presence of mind to keep her voice low. "They revel in their victory, thinking nothing of the mockery they have made of our family. How shall we ever endure such relations?"

"If you speak of mockery, Caroline," said Louisa, keeping her tone mild, "I believe you have already done a credible job of it yourself."

Caroline shot her a censorious look, but Louisa felt no need to indulge her sister at this late date. "Remember, Caroline — this business with Mr. Bennet was *your* doing and yours alone. There was never any chance of preventing Mr. Darcy and Charles from proposing to their chosen Bennet sisters, but *you* might have preserved yourself for a potential match to another gentleman in London. If you wish to rail against your fate look in the mirror — there you may apportion blame."

The mumble with which her sister replied was unintelligible and likely better it was so. Caroline looked away from her, refusing to give Louisa any more of her attention. But she would not escape so easily.

"Consider this, Caroline: you always wished to become the wife of a gentleman. Now you will be one.

"Before you attempt to denigrate Mr. Bennet's position," added Louisa when Caroline appeared ready to release some caustic reply, "remember that you will share his level of society."

"I wished to marry a gentleman," said Caroline, her tone the sulkiness of a child of six, "but not *this* gentleman. I was to be mistress of Pemberley."

"Therein you reveal your greatest failing. You aspired to be the mistress of Pemberley, but you thought nothing of Mr. Darcy. Do you suppose the gentleman appreciates being the object of interest for no other reason than his great estate? Is it at all surprising that Mr. Darcy chose the woman who treated him as if *he* was worthy in his own right, who gave no hint of coveting his position or his wealth? Look at her! Can you not see that she is as much in love with him as he is with her?"

For a long moment, Caroline watched them, fury etched on her brow. It would not have surprised Louisa had her sister persisted in her offense and indignation. Caroline said nothing, and after a moment, her displeasure crumpled along with her defiance.

"I suppose I might have gone about catching Mr. Darcy a different way."

"That much is evident."

A hint of fire again appeared in Caroline's eyes. "Love is not a prized commodity in marriage, Louisa. I did nothing that many other society ladies have done in attempting to capture a husband."

"In London, yes," replied Louisa, "though I will note that compromise is not an acceptable method of catching a husband to anyone of any sense."

Caroline had the grace to blush.

"It is apparent that Mr. Darcy is different," continued Louisa. "Yet, even if you behaved differently, I doubt Mr. Darcy would have given you what you desire. Little though you may wish to confess it, to my eyes it appears Mr. Darcy has found his heart's desire. You were never anything more than Charles's sister."

"I suppose you must be correct," muttered Caroline.

"It is good to hear you confess it," said Louisa. "Take my advice, Caroline. Perhaps this marriage is not what you wanted, but it is what you will have. Learn to be happy, for if you persist in bemoaning your fate, you will not be comfortable in your life."

Hoping her sister would listen to her advice, Louisa left her and approached the happy couples, giving them her congratulations. Louisa had no notion if Caroline would be happy, but for her sake and that of her future husband, she hoped they would reach some sort of accord.

CHAPTER XIV

*A*n accord did come, though it was a painful process. Mr. Bennet possessed no illusions as to Miss Bingley's lack of desire to be his wife, and the woman remained surly for some time after their hurried wedding.

Bennet maintained his patience and in time, her disposition mellowed. No genuine affection ever sprang up between them, but Bennet, keeping his philosophical bent, contented himself with the benefits marriage to his second wife brought. With a young wife, Mr. Bennet gained the chance to try again for an heir, and to his great joy, Mrs. Bennet presented him with three fine boys, accompanied by a little girl, which Bennet noted, sardonically, was not at all a surprise, considering his history. If Mr. Bennet overheard his wife teaching her daughter the evils of using underhanded means to capture a husband on several occasions, he could only feel gratitude that she had learned her lesson.

What Mrs. Bennet thought on the situation and how she coped were matters less simple in the understanding, for she did not vouchsafe her opinion to anyone, even those closest to her. What *was* true to anyone who cared to observe her was that she appeared to settle into her position with tolerable ease once she became accustomed to the changes in her life. If she did not appreciate the paucity of their visits to London, the lack of recognition she received, and, at times, the open disdain from those to whom she had previously boasted of her future as mistress of Pemberley, soon satisfied her of any desire to be there. After that, she contented herself with her position of prominence among the matrons of Meryton. That, of course, did not manifest itself until some years had passed and those worthy ladies forgot her slights against them.

What Mr. Collins thought about Mr. Bennet's three sons was not a matter of debate, for the man did not hesitate to share his opinion. Perhaps it was due to his wife's influence, for he did not carry his grudge to the end of his days, contenting himself with his parish and his patroness's attentions. Mr. Bennet appreciated the years of correspondence with his cousin, for he could always count on the parson to provide him with a measure of diversion with his silly observations.

Jane and Elizabeth Bennet, having become engaged on the same day, also married in the same ceremony, each achieving their lifelong ambition to marry for affection. After a time at Netherfield Park, Mr. Bingley resolved to seek his permanent home in the north, and with Mr. Darcy's assistance, he purchased an estate not twenty miles from Pemberley, fulfilling their wives' desire to be near each other. If the visits between the two women and their father were largely conducted in Hertfordshire, they all kept up the fiction that it was because of the Bingleys and Darcys' visits to town and the Bennet family's disinclination to travel to the north. Had Mr. Bennet not been busy with his sons, he might have taken to visiting them often and when least expected, but such visits did not take place until after his boys were grown, by which time he had attained a ripe old age.

The younger Bennet sisters also found a measure of happiness for themselves, each marrying men of property, though neither were so wealthy as Darcy and Bingley. It could be said that Mrs. Bennet settled further after the last of her stepdaughters quit their childhood home for good, but no one in the family recognized that fact. One connection the woman continued to disdain with no hint of surrender was the Gardiners, for she continued to detest any connection with trade. The Gardiners met her incivility with philosophy and accepted the distance, though Mr. Bennet and Mr. Gardiner remained in contact frequently. With Mr. Bennet's daughters, the Gardiners ever after remained on the closest of terms, the families often exchanging visits.

With the Hursts, the Bingleys remained close, though they were not in company with the rest of the family much. Darcy, as he had confided to Elizabeth, considered Hurst a bore and his wife uninteresting, and Elizabeth, though she could esteem Mrs. Hurst tolerably, had difficulty enduring her husband. With her sister, Mrs. Hurst remained on speaking terms, though their relations were not warm. Mrs. Bennet blamed her sister for her truthful words about her behavior, and Mrs. Hurst accepted her sister's acrimony, contenting herself with remaining at a distance.

Of Mr. Bennet's hasty marriage with Miss Bingley, they spoke little in future years. The die was cast, and the future decided, and he knew there was no reason to belabor the point. Secretly, Mr. Bennet thought on the matter, and after some time of this, he began to harbor certain suspicions about how the fateful evening had come about. In time, he found the opportunity to query his son-in-law.

"Your sons are certainly not quiet young men, Bennet."

Since arriving the previous day, the boys had caused no end of mischief, pulling Darcy's eldest in with their schemes, not unwillingly. Diverted by Darcy's observation, Bennet chuckled and shook his head. "No, they are not. In fact, I dare say the clamor they raise in my house is akin to what your wife caused." Bennet paused and considered his younger progeny. "Thomas is to go to Eton next year."

"Then the year after," said Darcy, "Bennet will join him."

Bennet was Darcy's eldest son, continuing the Darcy tradition of naming their eldest son with their mother's maiden name. Bennet Darcy was a year younger than Thomas Bennet, and the boys were thick as thieves, leading their younger siblings in mischief that would have made his cousin Fitzwilliam blush.

"Thomas cannot wait," replied Bennet. "But there is nothing to fear, for my son is bold, and shall have no trouble making friends at school."

"I would not have imagined he would," said Darcy, considering his brother-in-law's character, though considering a ten-year-old boy his brother was still a matter of some curiosity. Thomas had received more than a hint of the former Miss Bingley's brashness, though tempered by Bennet's retiring nature. By contrast, Bennet Darcy had received a measure of his mother's liveliness, though, again, Darcy's caution muted it to a certain extent.

For some more moments, they spoke of their families, their milestones and struggles. Unlike the Bennets, the Darcys had been blessed with two daughters and a son, and with Elizabeth showing signs of increasing yet again, Darcy had hope that the imbalance would be righted by the arrival of another boy.

Bennet, he noted with amusement, appeared content with what amounted to his second family, for he mentioned more than once how disinclined he was to father another child. His youngest, a daughter Mrs. Bennet had named Lydia, was now two years of age and an active child, one who chased her brothers about the house and yard, shrieking with laughter the entire time. His father-in-law, Darcy knew, did not appreciate the noise in his house.

The longer they spoke, however, the more Darcy realized his companion was distracted, though he could not say why. It certainly never crossed his mind that Bennet would raise the subject of the evening of the Netherfield ball, given more than ten years had passed since the event. At length, Bennet surprised him by doing exactly that.

"Darcy," said he, leaning forward with his elbows on his desk, his bright gaze fixed upon Darcy, "I have wished to ask you a question for some time now, yet I have never known how to raise the subject. For a time, I will own that I had intended to allow the matter to remain buried." The man chuckled and shook his head. "It is the curse of a curious man to wish to know everything, which is why I bring it up now.

"Thus, I ask you openly, since I doubt hesitancy will serve us—did you have anything to do with the events that led to my marriage?"

"Are you asking if I engineered the compromise?" asked Darcy carefully.

"Yes, if any such answer has meaning."

Darcy kept his mien carefully blank. "Why do you suppose *I* arranged it?"

"It all seemed too pat," said Bennet, not backing down an inch. "*You* were her target and yet she compromised *me*. An opportunistic man might have used that and the incidental resemblance between us to his advantage."

"I suppose he might have," said Darcy with a chuckle.

It was near impossible to determine Bennet's state of mind. That he was asking so openly and his words on the subject told Darcy that Bennet's suspicions had evolved over a lengthy period. Yet he did not appear to be angry, only curious. In the end, there was little reason to demur. Darcy had not thought of those events for some time, yet he cast his thoughts to the past and recalled what he had learned of that night.

"I do know what happened that night," confessed Darcy, "though I had nothing to do with seeing you compromised."

"Oh?" asked Bennet, arching a brow at him.

"I knew of Mrs. Bennet's intent to compromise me. Not only did I inform her of my refusal to pursue her as a prospective bride, but she requested the house keys from the housekeeper a few nights before the ball. My man, Snell, learned of it and took steps to prevent her, ensuring she knew what they were."

"He did?" Bennet's interest was piqued.

"He requested a cot and placed it not ten feet from the door to my chamber," said Darcy, provoking a guffaw from the other man. "It was amusing to watch her gnash her teeth in the evenings, knowing she wished to enter my bedchamber, but knowing Snell would not allow her to come within twenty-five feet of me."

"That must have provoked her desperation at the ball, then," observed Bennet.

"I dare say it did. But in all her scheming she did not account for Snell's determination to prevent her from claiming the position of mistress of my estate. In this, Snell feels he was acting in the interest of all my staff."

That provoked Bennet to mirth yet again. "Your man is an oddity, Darcy. But for all of that, he is a good sort of man."

"You are correct in both respects," agreed Darcy.

"Then he was the instigator of that evening's theatrics?"

"Not the instigator," said Darcy. "Mrs. Bennet initiated it. But Snell acted to thwart her intrigues. I was suspicious after the event, leading me to approach Snell to learn the truth. I apologize if you feel my silence was unwarranted, but I felt there was no reason to reopen old grievances."

"No reason except my curiosity," said Bennet.

Darcy nodded. "In reality, Snell's interference was small, though it had profound consequences for you. Miss Bingley instructed a footman to inform me that my valet wished to speak to me in the library. But Snell, having learned of it, approached the footman after and told him that he would wait in the parlor instead. He gave no reason for not summoning me himself, and the footman did not ask. Mrs. Bennet, it seemed, did not encourage the staff to question anything they were told."

At that, Bennet rolled his eyes. "Yes, I am familiar with that facet of my wife's management of the house. It took me several years to convince her of the worth of an intelligent servant."

"Whether Snell knew you were in the library I cannot say," continued Darcy. "He was not forthcoming on the subject. I suspect he did not know when he redirected me to the back parlor, else he might have simply allowed me to go to the library, knowing your wife could not compromise me in your company."

"Unless he wished to use the situation to ensure she was never in a position to become your wife," observed Bennet.

Darcy gave him a helpless shrug. "As I said, I do not know the truth of the matter, and I felt it was not worth it to order Snell to answer. As you said yourself, he is an oddity and more than a little prickly."

Bennet shook his head and chuckled, his usual amusement making an appearance. "Well, it was not what I thought, but I suspected there was some other hand in that business for several years."

"You are not angry?"

"As you said, it has been ten years. There is little enough reason to belabor the point at this late date.

"Besides, have I not benefited from your man's actions? Had Mrs. Bennet not compromised me, I would have remained a widower, and would not be, even now, training my son to become the master of the estate after I am gone. Caroline is not objectionable now that she has settled, and I have gained much more than I lost."

"Your cousin likely does not agree."

Bennet snorted. "I care little what my cousin thinks. Moreover, though he might not confess it, I suspect Collins is happier where he is. If he inherited Longbourn, he would bankrupt the estate in six months."

Darcy could not agree more. Bennet let the matter rest and moved on to other subjects. Darcy suspected they would never speak of it again.

That evening after they retired, Darcy lay down, his wife pressed up against his side. Thus it had been every night since their marriage, for they both delighted in the close contact and the closer relationship they had forged. Darcy spoke of her father's suspicions and their conversation that day in his study, and Elizabeth laughed at the matter again.

"Well, now that my father's curiosity is assuaged, I suspect he will be content with it."

"That is what I think," replied Darcy.

"In other circumstances," continued she, "I might have been angry with your valet. But my father is, in some ways, suited to the marriage he has with Charles's sister, though I could not have endured one similar."

"Then it is fortunate you do not need to," said Darcy, nuzzling her hair, pressing kisses to her temple.

"Aye, it is fortunate, indeed," murmured she, responding to his advances. "I must remember to thank Mr. Snell again, for he truly has done us a great service."

Further reply was impossible, for Darcy had no intention of letting her speak again for some time. In the back of his mind, he agreed with his wife. The compromise Snell had provoked was far more agreeable than the one Caroline Bennet had had in mind.

The End

MORE GREAT TITLES FROM
ONE GOOD SONNET PUBLISHING!

PRIDE AND PREJUDICE VARIATIONS

By Jann Rowland

Acting on Faith
A Life from the Ashes (Sequel to
Acting on Faith)
Open Your Eyes
Implacable Resentment
An Unlikely Friendship
Bound by Love
Cassandra
Obsession
Shadows Over Longbourn
The Mistress of Longbourn
My Brother's Keeper
Coincidence
The Angel of Longbourn
Chaos Comes to Kent
In the Wilds of Derbyshire
The Companion
Out of Obscurity
What Comes Between Cousins
A Tale of Two Courtships
Murder at Netherfield
Whispers of the Heart
A Gift for Elizabeth
Mr. Bennet Takes Charge

The Impulse of the Moment
The Challenge of Entail
A Matchmaking Mother
Another Proposal
With Love's Light Wings
Flight to Gretna Green
Mrs. Bennet's Favorite Daughter
Her Indomitable Resolve
Love and Libertine
In Default of Heirs Male
Among Intimate Acquaintances
Danger at the Netherfield Ball
More Agreeably Engaged
Unintended Consequences
An Agreeable Compromise

By Lelia Eye

Netherfield's Secret
A Sister's Sacrifice

By Colin Rowland

The Parson's Rescue
Hidden Desires
Disgraceful Conduct

PRIDE AND PREJUDICE SERIES

By Jann Rowland

COURAGE ALWAYS RISES: THE BENNET SAGA

The Heir's Disgrace
Volume II Untitled*
Volume III Untitled*

NO CAUSE TO REPINE

A Tacit Engagement
Scandalous Falsehoods
Upstart Pretensions
Quitting the Sphere
No Cause to Repine Box Set

BONDS OF LIFE

Bonds of Friendship
Bonds of Love

* Forthcoming

OTHER GENRES BY
ONE GOOD SONNET PUBLISHING

FANTASY

By Jann Rowland & Lelia Eye

EARTH AND SKY SERIES

On Wings of Air
On Lonely Paths
*On Tides of Fate**

FAIRYTALE

By Lelia Eye

The Princes and the Peas: A Tale of Robin Hood

SMOTHERED ROSE TRILOGY

Thorny
Unsoiled
Roseblood

* Forthcoming

About the Author

Jann Rowland

Jann Rowland is a Canadian, born and bred. Other than a two-year span in which he lived in Japan, he has been a resident of the Great White North his entire life, though he professes to still hate the winters.

Though Jann did not start writing until his mid-twenties, writing has grown from a hobby to an all-consuming passion. His interests as a child were almost exclusively centered on the exotic fantasy worlds of Tolkien and Eddings, among a host of others. As an adult, his interests have grown to include historical fiction and romance, with a particular focus on the works of Jane Austen.

When Jann is not writing, he enjoys rooting for his favorite sports teams. He is also a master musician (in his own mind) who enjoys playing piano and singing as well as moonlighting as the choir director in his church's congregation.

Jann lives in Alberta with his wife of more than twenty years, two grown sons, and one young daughter. He is convinced that whatever hair he has left will be entirely gone by the time his little girl hits her teenage years. Sadly, though he has told his daughter repeatedly that she is not allowed to grow up, she continues to ignore him.

Please let him know what you think or sign up for their mailing list to learn about future publications:

Website: http://onegoodsonnet.com/
Facebook: https://facebook.com/OneGoodSonnetPublishing/
Twitter: **@OneGoodSonnet**
Mailing List: http://eepurl.com/bol2p9

Made in the USA
Monee, IL
26 December 2022

23683884R00094